Flames of Murder

A.M. Holloway

Published By:

Your Book Company

eBook ISBN: 978-1-7359152-6-5

Paper ISBN: 978-1-7359152-7-2

Library of Congress Control Number: 2021910369

Printed in the United States of America.

Prologue

Flames rise high into the night air. Fueled by a gusty breeze, the blaze dances across the rooftop, consuming every store in its path. One by one, the fire destroys an entire shopping center, just missing the office park beside it. A few of the owners opened their doors in this exact location thirty years ago, making this shopping center one of the first in the area. This loss is a devastating blow to the community, but the people always come together in a crisis.

The fire department arrives at the scene within minutes of the 911 call and quickly assesses the situation. At this time of night, the stores are empty of customers, saving valuable time. The first responders gather equipment, preparing to enter the stores when the first bullet cuts through the inferno, striking a tree beside the fire engine. Everyone seeks cover behind the fire trucks suspecting more bullets will follow. As the wind whips, the fire rages, sending flames higher into the air. Flying bullets pin the firefighters behind their trucks, and all they can do is watch the show until the ladder truck douses the gun shop fire from above, cooling left-over embers and ammunition. With the gun store cooled, the firefighters extinguish the flames in the remaining stores. Once the fire is out, all that remains is a gutted shell where it began its torment.

When morning comes and the sun rises, two fire investigators walk through the remnants of the gun shop, searching for the fire's origin. Although accustomed to walking through burned rubble, the fire's source stumps the investigators. The duo continue their search, marking several areas of interest. Typically, a point of origin is confined to one area, but this fire appears to have started in several areas.

As the investigators continue their inspection, the arsonist watches the show from across the street, wondering if the investigators are smart enough to find him and the origin. He smiles.

Chapter 1

Mac walks towards the conference room in the FBI Atlanta field office. She eyes Spencer leaning on the wall, talking into his cell phone. He is unaware of Mac's approach. Mac touches his arm on the way by, and Spencer almost drops his phone. The eye contact is unmistakable. *Why that look?* Mac thinks to herself. *Is Spencer mad about something?* Mac could remember saying nothing out of line to him.

Two seats closest to the door remain vacant. Mac sits in one, eager for the meeting to end. Spencer enters the conference room and slides into the chair next to Mac without glancing her way. His eyes focused on the front of the room.

SAC Williams delivers the meeting notes in his standard form. The office continues to handle multiple high-profile cases, with every agent in the room working on one. Mac and Spencer are the next team up for an assignment.

After solving their last case and being cleared by internal affairs, Mac is glad to be back at work. The FBI relieved her of duty while internal affairs investigated the deadly accident of an alleged serial killer—a man who wanted Mac dead. The killer murdered other FBI agents in cold blood, and he perished in a vehicle accident involving Mac and Spencer.

While it's nice being back at work, the vacation was excellent too. Two weeks away from the job's hustle and bustle was much needed, and to top it off, Spencer tagged along. They talked about their future, both work and personal. Mac knows Spencer loves her, and she loves him. However, they made no decisions about their future together. Both are content with the relationship as it stands, and Mac doesn't want to jeopardize her position at the bureau with her career just getting started.

Once the meeting concludes, Mac and Spencer discuss the overnight gun store fire. The morning headlines broadcast the news about the fire, and both agents heard it. The FBI still has an interest in the owner. Mac follows Spencer to Agent Williams' office. They advise Agent Williams of their intent to visit the scene this morning, hoping to speak with the investigator in charge.

Agent Williams wonders why the team wants to visit the store, but since they have no fresh cases, he doesn't stop them. The fire intrigues him, too. Hunter Bows has been a topic around the FBI for years. It would be nice to pin something on him once and for all.

The duo climbs into Spencer's SUV, and he drives them to the gun store for a look around. He ponders why someone would torch the store at night when it was unoccupied. Spencer visited the gun store months ago during a prior investigation, and he recalled the security system was outstanding. The alarm connected directly to the 911 system. Spencer wondered what kept them from extinguishing the fire more quickly.

Upon their arrival at the scene, emergency vehicles still fill the parking lot, but they squeeze their car next to a curb. Spencer takes the lead, and Mac follows as he introduces them to the lead fire investigator, Tyrone Gutherie. Tyrone is a man's man. With short-cropped hair, he stands 6'7", 320 pounds, and he is hard as a rock. The white button-down shirt sleeve rides up his arm as he points at the gun store, and Mac glimpses the same tattoo her dad wears on his forearm.

Tyrone gives them the rundown on the fire. The owner inspected the store last night, and he is at headquarters now, answering a few more questions. Then Tyrone asks, "What brings the FBI by?"

Spencer explains, "The FBI investigated the store owner, Hunter Bows, in the past for transporting weapons across the border into Mexico. We are curious if the old investigation is rearing its ugly head or if this fire was accidental. Do you know what started it?"

"It took twelve hours to figure out a source for the fire. Bombs and fires have been my life since graduating from high school and joining the service. I won't stop until I find the origin, although it might take time. This fire started with a lot of gasoline. I guess somebody used the old-fashioned Molotov cocktail to start it, which is the only way the perpetrator escaped without injury. This fire was furious, and for it to be scorching at that hour, the flame had help, and gasoline was the help it needed." Tyrone continues, "With the ammunition stored inside the gun shop, the first responders couldn't gain entry for fear of being shot."

Spencer nods his head as he realizes the store's ammunition delayed the firefighter's response in extinguishing the flames. He glances at the damaged store.

Mac speaks up next. "If you hear anything useful from the owner, will you share the information? It might be helpful to us." Tyrone stares at Mac with a flash of recognition, and Spencer questions him about it.

"Tyrone, why are you staring at Mac that way? Do you two know each other?" Spencer questions with his eyebrows together.

"I've never met him until now," Mac explains with a sharp tone in her voice.

Tyrone shakes his head as if he has cobwebs. "Sorry, guys, but Mac, you look familiar, and you remind me of someone. What is your full name? If you don't mind me asking."

"Mackenzie Morris, but everyone calls me Mac. Why?" Mac questions with a head tilt.

"I swear, I've met you. You seem familiar, somehow, but I don't recognize your name. Oh well, back to work." Tyrone shakes his head, trying to put the pieces together.

Mac pauses before she asks Tyrone a question. "May I ask a question of you?" Tyrone nods his head in agreement. "I saw your tattoo earlier. You wouldn't know, Myles Morris, would you?"

"Have mercy, girl. Myles is your dad! I knew it, I know you! I served with your dad in the service on tour, and then they shipped me to another unit that needed a bomb guy. If your daddy is still with us, I would love to speak to him. Can you have him call me sometime?" Tyrone passes Mac a few of his business cards with a smile. Mac notices how his smile lights up his face.

"It will be my pleasure, Tyrone. How fascinating to meet someone that served with Dad! I can't wait to share the news with him." Mac smiles as she glances at Spencer and Tyrone.

Their newfound friend, Tyrone, hands the duo booties and face masks, and then he gives them the tour of the torched gun shop. They trample through parched rubble and half-burned ceiling joists until Tyrone stops at a spot on the right side of the store. This side of the store faces the woods at the end of the shopping center. "Look at this." Tyrone lifts a large piece of timber and points at a wad of something on the floor. "This is plastic from a gas can, I'm guessing. Our lab techs are running the composite tests on it now. If my hunch is correct, someone filled the gas cans with gasoline, inserted a rag or towel into the spout, lit it on fire, threw it on top of the building, and ran away."

Spencer looks at Tyrone, "I haven't heard of those in years." Spencer shakes his head in disbelief.

"That's what I'm thinking, anyway. It would explain how the flames spread across the roof of the store. The wind swept the flames across the remaining stores. That part is explainable." Tyrone's eyes continuously rove over the area to make sure he has missed nothing. "Look around. This area is not stable, with ceiling parts falling, so be careful. I'm returning to headquarters to visit with the owner. I'll let you know what he offers. If you have any further questions, please call, and I look forward to hearing from your dad." Tyrone reaches out, and they shake hands as they bid him farewell.

"Can you believe he served with dad, Spencer? What are the odds? This is a first for me." Mac stares at Tyrone's business card as she ponders the meeting.

Spencer grins as he looks at Mac. "You're glowing, you're so excited. It looks good on you. I can't imagine the odds of you meeting a service member of your dad's either. I hope your dad is as happy as you are."

"What's that supposed to mean? Why wouldn't Dad be glad to hear from Tyrone?" Mac quips.

"I don't know. I've never been in the service, but I've always heard service members stay in close contact with those they serve beside. He might be just as happy as you. In fact, I hope he is."

Mac hopes it will delight her dad to hear from Tyrone. She'll tell him tonight over supper. Maybe her dad will share some of his military stories about Tyrone. He seems like one of the good guys, and Mac still loves the stories.

Spencer and Mac walk back to their car, smelling like smokestacks. "I hate fires. The smell permeates everything it touches." Mac slips out of her jacket and places it on the back seat of the car. "What do you think, Spencer? Did the owner poke the wrong guy?"

"I'm not sure what to think. When we get back to the office, let's peruse the old case files. Drake handled the investigation so those files will be meticulous." As soon as Spencer mentions

Drake's name, Mac's facial expression changes and not for the better. "I'm sorry. I shouldn't have brought his name up yet."

"Don't worry about it. It felt good not to think of Drake. We can't work here without hearing his name. I have wondered where he landed after the debacle with Seth." Mac ponders ideas of Drake's whereabouts. She doesn't want to live the rest of her life looking over her shoulder, but she will until Drake shows himself.

It takes two trips from the evidence room to get all twenty boxes of Drake's investigation records upstairs to Mac and Spencer's conference room. "Based on the number of boxes, Drake was thorough in his investigation. I'm unsure why nothing transpired from it. With this many boxes, you would think the guy is guilty of something."

"There is no telling what these boxes hold. We can start from the beginning and work our way to the present." Spencer slices the evidence tape with a razor knife and signs the form, proving he did the deed.

They sort the files in chronological order, and then they begin with one file at a time. Mac writes pertinent information on the whiteboard, and as they gather more, they add to it.

With hours of reading behind them, Mac announces she's going to her parents for supper. Spencer shares he has plans with his family too. Mac doesn't like to intrude on Spencer's family time since he doesn't see them often. Mac and Spencer know they will talk again before bedtime.

Neither one wants to go to sleep without talking to the other one last time.

With the smell of smoke lingering on her clothes and hair, Mac stops by her midtown Atlanta apartment for a shower before visiting her parents. With the workday over, her excitement about sharing her meeting with Tyrone grows.

Chapter 2

During supper, Mac shares her day with her parents, topping it off with meeting Tyrone at the fire. Myles, Mac's dad, could not believe she met an old fellow service member at a local fire scene. Myles' face lit up when he thought back to his military days, and the memories of Tyrone came flooding into his mind. The stories Myles told about Tyrone and his bravery were amazing. The men lost track of each other when Tyrone shipped to another unit on the opposite side of the world. With Tyrone's business card in hand, Myles slips away from the girls so he can make the call.

An hour later, Myles reappears with a grin on his face, expressing his gratitude to Mac for getting Tyrone's number. Myles and Tyrone agree to meet for lunch soon. Myles asks Mac, "Where did you meet Tyrone? I didn't know you and Spencer handle fire investigations."

"Tyrone is the lead fire investigator on the gun store fire in south Fulton. The FBI investigated the owner for smuggling weapons into Mexico, and the store burned to the ground overnight. Drake handled the investigation, but nothing ever came of it. So, Spencer and I are recreating Drake's investigation. We pulled twenty boxes from the evidence room and started at the beginning. It might be a waste of time, but the fire appears to have started with a Molotov cocktail using gallon jugs and gasoline. With the cocktail, it was deliberate. Someone had their sights set on harming the gun store." Mac watches her dad process the information. Myles knows something about this gun store, but what?

The silence continues as Myles processes the information received. "Would the owner's name be Hunter Bows? If so, we investigated him years ago too. The ATF asked for our help since they were short on resources. Hunter was under surveillance twenty-four hours a day for a few weeks, and I would swear he knew it. He was almost too careful. That investigation was one of the most frustrating cases that involved me since I opened my firm."

"Yes, that's the gun store owner's name. The FBI uncovered no wrongdoing, so I am assuming you didn't either. Right?" Mac looks at her dad with an eyebrow lifted.

"That's right. Hunter had late-night visitors at his home and the store, but the visitors checked out as legit gun buyers. We pinned nothing on him, even though some things were shady. We never understood why gun buyers dropped by in the middle of the night to pick up their purchases."

After talking with her dad, Mac leaves for her apartment. She looks forward to a good night's sleep because they will face a mound of reading tomorrow. Mac calls Spencer while driving home to tell him about her dad investigating Hunter Bows alongside the ATF. It shocks Spencer to learn of her dad's involvement. Emergency vehicles speed past Mac, and Spencer mentions the noise. So, she turns on her scanner, hoping she'll overhear details about the situation. After the scanner beeps several times, the dispatcher tones for another fire department to respond to a house fire. Mac explains the sirens and the house fire to Spencer, and their call ends.

With this new connection, Mac's curiosity about Hunter Bows peaks. She backs her vehicle into her assigned slot and walks into her apartment, wondering what Hunter Bows is hiding and if they have a fresh case. Mac scours her apartment for something to take her mind off of Hunter, but nothing works, so she heads to bed. Her mind continues on its mind bending path until her alarm blares.

After a quick breakfast, she readies herself for the day. Her drive to the office wasn't half bad, since traffic was on her side for once. The bright morning sun shines through the FBI Atlanta field office's windows as Mac enters the conference room. She raises her hand to shield her eyes. "How can you see anything in here? The reflection is incredible." Mac stops speaking when she realizes Spencer is standing at the window on his phone.

Spencer ends his call, walks over, and sits in his chair without making eye contact with Mac. Then he states, "You know I like sunshine. It will pass soon. Give it time. I've been here for an hour, and this case file is nothing more than notes taken by agents looking to make overtime pay. The FBI surveilled Hunter Bows for four weeks, two years ago. He went to work at the same time every day, mid-morning he made a bank deposit, and left for home around 5:00 pm. Sometimes, he would come back to the store later at night if he had a visitor, or the visitor would drop by his house."

"What do we know about the visitors? Any of them stand out as criminals or gang members?" Mac stares at Spencer while she speaks, wondering what is on his mind. She feels something is slipping in their relationship.

Spencer turns a page in a file and glances up at Mac. "None that I can find. Drake and his team ran backgrounds on the gun buyers, and nothing transpired from them." Spencer's attention returns to his file.

Scenarios play out for Mac, but nothing sticks. "This gun store owner was diligent in his schedule. What does that tell us? Not one thing. Maybe we have nothing on him. But, if he is clean, why would someone torch his store?"

A few hours later, twenty now empty boxes sit against the conference room walls, and there isn't much written on the whiteboard. Spencer and Mac understand why the FBI didn't press charges against Hunter Bows for transporting weapons. The only person who knew of the transactions was a confidential informant, and he's been missing for over a year. The FBI never found the informant's body. Without the body, they had no evidence to support Hunter's arrest.

"You know, Spencer, Dad didn't mention an informant being involved with this guy. I wonder if he knew about it, and if he did, why didn't he tell me about it?"

Without an answer, Spencer shrugs his shoulders and finishes reading the last file on Hunter Bows. "There was a cause for suspicion over the comings and goings of Hunter Bows, but without hard evidence, no one gathered enough evidence to convict him. My question is money. How did he make his money? Foot traffic in the store wasn't great, but his sales were high. I suggest we tackle his financials after lunch."

"How about going to Roy's diner? We haven't been there in a while. I'll drive." Mac asks.

"You drove to lunch yesterday. It's my turn. Besides, you need to call your dad and ask about the confidential informant. It would interest us to hear if he knew anything about it."

Mac agrees, and they take the elevator down to the lobby and exit the building, heading into the bright Atlanta sunshine. The city is gearing up for a lot of foot traffic this weekend. The Braves are in town with a concert scheduled at the same time. Even though the Braves moved their facilities north of the city, fans still stay in downtown Atlanta, creating a traffic nightmare.

Roy's Diner has been in business for decades, and Roy still runs the day-to-day operations. He involves his kids and grandkids in a variety of ways. The food is delicious, with hamburgers so juicy that it will run down your arms if you're not careful. But the effort to protect clothes is worth it. Halfway through their meal, a breaking news bulletin appears on the TV, showing a house fire in Fulton County. Mac and Spencer glance at the TV while continuing to eat. It was not until the news reporter said four words, "Hunter and Caroline Bows," that Spencer and Mac pay attention to the story. Overnight, the Bows perished in a house fire. The Fulton County fire investigators are on the scene, and more information will follow on tonight's broadcast. The couple shared a nod and wiped their hands and mouths with napkins. They knew they had swallowed their last bite of lunch.

Chapter 3

Cash lands on the table from two different hands, covering the bill at Roy's Diner, as Mac and Spencer sprint for the car. With Spencer behind the wheel, Mac calls the office for the home address of Hunter Bows. After she ends the call, she looks at Spencer with her eyebrows raised. "This house fire was the one on the scanner last night. The emergency vehicles were traveling in that direction. I should have followed them. We would have seen it firsthand."

"You didn't know it was their house. Don't beat yourself up over it. You wouldn't have seen much in the pitch darkness, anyway. We'll have time to look around now," Spencer counters as he maneuvers through traffic.

Hunter's subdivision is older than Mac expected. However, it is still posh even with the smaller lot size. The home's exterior is typical of the year built, but the outdoor living space that graces the backyard is modern and incredible. The deck boasts tiers of decking set with massive planters filled to the brim with flowers sitting along the edges. Fragrance from the flowers permeates the air, with some smells sweeter than others. Hunter, like his neighbors, has a massive outdoor fireplace and kitchen, swimming pool, and a hot tub. As Mac surveys the surroundings, she sees how easy it would be to enter the backyard without being seen.

Each home has a wooden privacy fence, even though you can see into the neighbor's yard while standing on a deck. They spent a lot of money on a privacy fence that doesn't provide privacy from above. Maybe the owners felt it added a layer of security. After taking in the neighborhood's layout, Mac finds Tyrone leaning over his car's hood, looking at pieces of charred wood. She walks over. "Hey Tyrone, what are you looking at?"

"Hey, Mac. What brings you here? Or, actually, I should ask, what took you so long to get here?" Tyrone's bright white teeth gleam in the sun.

"We were having lunch, and a breaking news bulletin jarred us into action. So, what can you tell me about this fire?" Mac asks as she wonders why Tyrone did not call her about the fire.

"I can tell you what I know, which is not much. The fire started around eleven last night. A neighbor went to the kitchen for something to drink and saw the flames. The fire department responded within minutes of the call, and they were dousing the fire when a car inside the garage exploded. After the explosion, another call went out for more firefighters because of the proximity of the homes. Upon entering the house, which was difficult because of the steel doors, the firefighters found Hunter and Caroline Bows deceased in their upstairs bedroom. The cause of death might be asphyxiation from the smoke, but I can't confirm. The medical examiner will determine the cause of death since there were no visible signs of trauma."

Mac glances at the house. "Why would a residential home have steel doors? Doesn't that seem odd to you, Tyrone?"

"Yes, it does. I asked myself that question. It sounds to me like something. or someone scared them." Tyrone turns his head at the new arrivals.

"So, I see ATF are here now. What brings them by?" Mac asks as she points in their direction.

Tyrone looks over at the ATF agents and says, "They are investigating whether this house fire connects to his store fire, as both appear intentional."

"I agree because first the store fire, now the home fire. That is way too close to be accidental. What about Hunter's interrogation? Did he reveal anything of interest to you?"

"Not a thing. Hunter emphasized he doesn't have enemies and has received no threats. We questioned him about his customers, but he said his customers loved his service. Hunter never explained what type of services he offers other than firearms. So, we got nothing to work with from him. He was in and out of the police department within two hours, and he never asked for an attorney."

Spencer walks over and asks Tyrone if the firebug used a Molotov cocktail again since both fires appear connected.

Pausing before he answers, Tyrone stammers, "I can't answer that yet. There is no melted plastic jug residue, no evidence of any kind. When the gas tank exploded, it destroyed everything in its path." Tyrone glances at the house like he is willing some additional evidence to come forth.

"That is no good, Tyrone. Isn't there some ash test the ATF can run for us? I remember a discussion about it at Quantico." Mac suggests in a hopeful tone.

Tyrone nods his head yes as he explains, "ATF is testing the ash now along with our techs. The only definitive fact I can say with any certainty is that the fire started outside the garage wall. The burn area covers a lot of ground, so that will take time."

Spencer continues, "At least that's something, Tyrone. There is a reason Hunter's house burned two days after his store burned. What about a car? Did one start the fire?"

"No. We ruled the cars out first. Besides, the origin was outside the garage on the back wall. There was dark-colored plastic melted together that matches the neighbor's trash can. We are assuming Hunter used the same trash collection service. If it is a trash container, someone started a fire in the can, and it torched the place. Whatever the contents were, they grew in intensity the longer they were in the can. Once the tests come back, I can give you a definite answer to your question."

Mac and Spencer look at each other as Tyrone makes his statement about the fire. People gather across the street from the burned house. Mac walks over to the group and asks if anyone saw or heard anything suspicious. No one offers even a tidbit of information. Everyone claims to have been asleep at the time the fire began.

While Mac is with the group, Spencer speaks with an officer at the scene. The officer confirms the department has not responded to any calls at the Bows' address. He can't fathom why the house and the store burned within days of each other. Much to Spencer's surprise, the officer states this is no accident. As Spencer walks away, he glances back at the police officer, wondering how he knew that the fire was no accident.

Spencer shares the officer's opinions, and Mac agrees with him. She doesn't think this is accidental, either. Whoever started this house fire did the same at the gun store, and now they are facing two counts of murder.

Their tour ends at the car, and Mac, wearing a puzzled expression, surveys the scene again. "Do you think this is gang-related? I've never worked in gangs, but with the weapons involved, I question the motive."

Spencer replies, "It neither looks nor feels like gangs. Both fires occurred in the middle of the night, all without grandstanding. Most of your gangs will want to show off in some manner because they have to prove their worth."

While sitting in the car, they ponder reasons for the two fires. Odds are, because the gun store fire started with a Molotov, the house fire was also intentional, although the cause is unknown. The question is, did the fire-setter know the victims were inside, or were they the target all along? Did the same person torch the house and store?

Mac and Spencer spend the rest of the day thumbing through the case files again. They agree there is nothing to tie the two fires together except the owner. If they can't find some correlation between the two, the FBI doesn't have a case—again.

A cell phone rings in the conference room, and Mac scrambles to find it. She knows her ringtone, but not where she left her phone. On the last ring, she snags it from under a pile of paper.

Mac's dad, Myles, calls for an update on the Hunter Bows case. Mac explains the FBI has no case because they can't tie the two fires together. She brings up the confidential informant. Myles denies knowing anything about a confidential informant. Mac questions him about his interest in this case. "I went back and reviewed my case files to make sure this is the same guy I thought it was, and it is. This guy is or was shady, but no one could pin anything on him. Then, I reviewed the newspaper files and found an article that a reporter wrote about a drive-by shooting in April. The police arrested the shooter over Memorial Day weekend. Hunter Bows's gun store sold the gun used in the drive-by."

Chapter 4

With additional information about the drive-by shooting, Mac informs Spencer she wants to dig deeper into it, hoping it will give them a fresh lead on the fires. Because the police are handling the shooting investigation, the FBI still doesn't have a case. Yet undeterred, Mac asks for Spencer's help in securing the police report on the drive-by shooting. He can't refuse her, so he makes a call.

While waiting for the police report, Mac dissects several scenarios between the shooting and the fires. The gun store owner is the only correlation. Mac shakes her head as pieces don't fit her puzzle. If the pieces don't fit, Mac moves them to the side. She never throws away a piece of information until they solve the case.

A few minutes later, Spencer hands Mac a copy of the police report. Both read the report, looking for a tie between the shooter and Hunter. The alleged shooter told the investigators he didn't know Mr. Bows, and he didn't shoot the gun. The shooter also commented that the shooting victims are unknown to him. It was a case of the wrong place at the wrong time for the victims.

"I want to interview the alleged shooter, Spencer. We need to find out what he knows. If he didn't shoot the gun, then who did, and why was he arrested as the shooter? Who knows, the gun purchase might have been legal, and then the gun might have been stolen. I see no information on the gun listed here. Do you have it?"

"Yes, I'm pulling the report on the serial number now. Here it is. Luther Evans of Atlanta purchased the gun. Then he reported it stolen a year later. Want to speak with Mr. Evans?"

"Mr. Evans will be a great place to start, even if someone stole the gun. Then, I would like to have a visit with our shooter. I hope he is still in the Fulton County lock-up. That's a simple visit instead of the Atlanta prison or down in Jackson."

"The records have our shooter registered in the Fulton County jail. Where do we start, shooter or gun buyer?"

Mac thinks for a moment. "Call Mr. Evans and see if he's available. If he is, we'll start there. We know where the shooter is when we need him."

Spencer picks up his phone and dials Mr. Evans. There was no answer, so he leaves a voicemail asking for a return call. "Since we can't meet Mr. Evans, we'll go to the jail and drop in on our shooter."

"If we are lucky, Mr. Evans will call back, and we can see him while we are out. I've got the police report if we need to refer to it." Mac plucks the report from her desk as she stands to leave.

Thirty minutes later, Mac and Spencer walk into the Fulton County jail. They check in with the desk Sargent and deposit their weapons in a locker. Every time Mac visits an inmate, her whole-body shivers. If there is anything that gives her the creeps, this is it. The smells and the noise are enough to drive a sane person crazy. After passing through several checkpoints, another officer leads them to a table sitting in the middle of a small rectangular room. The room color is gray, as are the table and chairs. When Mac sits in a chair, a draft of air blows past her neck, creating chill bumps on her arms. It gives a sensation that she needs to look over her shoulder to make sure no one is standing behind her.

Seconds later, an officer escorts the detainee into the interview room. They fasten the inmate to the table from the shackles he wears, and then the bolts slide as the door closes. The sound is unmistakable.

Mac catches herself staring at this guy. He is much younger than expected, a light-skinned African-American male with a short afro haircut. He is without visual markings—no piercings and no tattoos. This guy is a clean-cut kid. She just thought this shooter would sport gang tats, long hair, and not look like your neighbor's kid.

Spencer takes the lead with the questions. The kid is eager to talk, which is odd. Typical inmates keep their mouths shut for fear of retaliation. "What's your name?"

"Willie Simmons, Sir."

Mac glances at Spencer when she notices the kid has manners. "How old are you, Willie?"

Willie looks back and forth from Spencer to Mac, "17."

With the police report in his hand, Spencer asks Willie to describe the basketball court shooting. Willie's eyes shift from Mac to Spencer.

The conversation pauses as Willie realizes why the two FBI agents are here to visit. "I was a passenger in the vehicle when the shooting happened. I did NOT pull the trigger. Someone must believe me. No one told me what was going down that day."

Mac steps in. "Who was driving, Willie? We can't help you if you don't tell us."

Willie all but shrinks into himself. He clams up, and his eyes turn down.

With Willie thinking about his future, Spencer and Mac watch as he works out a plan. His eyes dart back and forth as he takes a deep breath.

At last, Mac asks Willie, "How long have you been in here?"

"Too long, ma'am. The police arrested me over Memorial Day weekend. I didn't even know they were looking for me until they picked me up walking home from the store."

"Have you discussed the shooting with anyone?"

"No, ma'am. Not since the day they brought me to the police station. I stayed there for a few days, and then they brought me here. I think I'm supposed to get a phone call or something, but I haven't spoken to anyone but you two." Willie's leg bounces up and down.

Mac's face turns red as she contains her temper. How could a police detective arrest a kid on a murder charge and not explain the process clearly enough to where he understands it? "Spencer and I are working on another case, and we need to know if you know anyone named Hunter Bows. He owns the Atlanta gun store where someone purchased the gun that was used in the drive-by shooting."

"I don't know anyone with that name. Like I said, I was a passenger in the car. Guns are not my thing. I've only shot one time, and it wasn't the drive-by." Willie states.

"Willie, please consider telling us who was driving the car that day. Don't waste your life on someone who doesn't care about yours. Here is my card. Call me when you're ready to talk. I'll be waiting." Mac hands her business card to Willie.

With that, Mac and Spencer leave the jail with no more information than when they arrived. Mac turns to Spencer. "He didn't pull that trigger. Who is he protecting, and why?"

"I agree with you, Mac, but we can't force the kid to tell us anything. He has your card. It is up to him now. Give him a few days. Let's see what happens. We can always stop in over here."

In the car, Mac and Spencer jot notes in their notebooks. Spencer retrieves a voicemail message from Luther Evans. He dials Luther's number. When he answers, Mac and Spencer ask a few questions, but it's obvious he is not the firebug. He purchased the gun from Hunter's store. Luther states he didn't know Hunter before that exchange. As soon as they end the call, Spencer's cell phone rings, and he glances at the caller ID before he answers the call from Williams.

Spencer listens to Williams deliver a brief message to return to headquarters, but he doesn't offer a reason.

"Did he give any details on why? Could he already know about our trip to the jail?"

"He didn't share, and I didn't ask. Williams has this tone in his voice that has me keeping my mouth shut. We will hear shortly." Spencer explains.

The duo makes the trip to the FBI office in silence. Each rationalizes the need to meet with Williams. He sits behind his desk, staring at a file with his eyebrows bunched together. "Sir, Spencer said you called for us," Mac says as she pokes her head into his office.

"Have a seat. We have a case, and I want you two to be the lead agents on it. It spans multiple states. There have been three new gun store fires, and the owners' homes were targets, just like Hunter Bows. The gun stores were in Tennessee, Kentucky, and Ohio."

Chapter 5

Agent Williams discusses the fires, including information received from his boss. FBI and ATF are creating a joint task force, and the FBI Atlanta Field Office is the home base for the investigation. While in the meeting, Mac and Spencer write copious notes on the newest fires' locations, both store and owner addresses. They share with Williams about their jail visit to meet the alleged shooter and their belief the incarcerated guy is not the firebug, which they can confirm since the suspected shooter is in jail, and the fires continue.

Once their meeting concludes, Mac and Spencer walk to their desks with their heads spinning. Mac pulls out the whiteboard and begins writing information on it for the case file.

"Spencer, can we attach a map to the wall? I'd like to pinpoint the location of the fires. A visual always helps me."

"Good idea. The three latest fires are in three different states north of Atlanta on Interstate 75. If I map the gun stores addresses, they were all close to the interstate, within two miles. However, the owners' homes are in outlying surrounding areas. I'm guessing here, but it looks like the furthest is five miles from the interstate."

The dry erase marker flies across the board as Mac writes. "Wonder why someone targeted these gun stores? Is the fire-setter looking for an easy getaway? But, if they were, why set fires to the owners' residence? With the distance to the interstate from the homes, it would make escaping a lot gutsier."

Spencer pins a United States map to a corkboard and sets push pins into the map, signifying the burned gun stores and the owners' homes. The gun stores sport yellow push pins, and the owners' homes have red. Push pins dot the map, but unfortunately, they expect to add more in the coming days. Spencer reads from his notes as Mac continues to write.

"After the Atlanta fires, Knoxville, Tennessee, followed. It occurred three days after the Atlanta fire took the lives of Hunter and Caroline Bows. The freestanding store burned first. The store was in business for decades and was owned by the same family. Two days later, the gun store owners' home burned to the ground. The owners, Rob and Sally Olson, were away on vacation. They declined police protection upon their return to town.

Lexington, Kentucky, was the next stopping place for the arsonist. The torched gun store was an end unit of a large shopping center, and it sustained substantial damage. The sprinklers kicked in and helped the firefighters knock down the flames. However, the water used to douse the flames caused extensive damage to the gun store and the adjoining store. Three days later, the owners, Henry and Harriett O'Brien, were the target of a fire. They escaped injury, and their house only charred. The weather helped save it because a rainstorm moved in shortly after the fire started.

Cincinnati, Ohio, was the scene of the third fire. The gun store occupied a freestanding building, which included a firing range in the back. Carter Pike, the owner, had recently purchased the store. The gun store provided a new career after retiring from the Army. When the store fire broke out, Carter was at home, and a local law enforcement officer stopped by and told him of the fire. He drove to the store and watched it burn. When the police learned of the other gun store fires, they conducted a three day stakeout of Carter's home. When nothing happened, the police assumed the arsonist moved on to another location. Five days after the store fire and two days after surveillance concluded, Carter's house burned to the ground with him inside.

Mac questions the information on the last fire. "Are you saying the police watched the owner's home for three days, surveillance stops, then two days later, the arsonist sets the owner's home on fire and kills Carter Pike?" Mac shakes her head as if she can't believe it.

"Yes, that's what the report shows. I see where you are going with this. If the arsonist were watching the house, he would know when the surveillance team left."

"Spencer, what do you think about requesting Tyrone Gutherie to be a member of this task force? His knowledge might prove invaluable. We need to find out what started the house fires."

"I agree. I'll let Williams know to make it happen." Spencer writes a reminder to himself.

"This discovery of the arsonist watching the owner's homes before torching them is terrifying. It makes me wonder if this guy is targeting the gun store owners. Now, he's murdered three. How many will it be before we catch this guy?" Mac shivers, thinking about the arsonist watching the owners' home before torching them.

"The report states a Molotov caused all the gun store fires. So far, the house fires are undetectable. We need to follow up with Tyrone on the Atlanta fires, anyway. Maybe he can help us with these others when he gets here."

Williams walks into the conference room with the ATF agents in tow. He introduces Mac and Spencer to the guys, and Spencer asks Williams about Tyrone joining the task force. Williams pauses, then agrees to make the call.

José Perez and Bradley T. Runcan appear to be likable guys. Mac glances at both while they chat with Spencer. José is short, stocky, with dark-colored hair. Bradley is the opposite. He is African-American, tall, and lean. Two opposites, as partners, make an interesting combination.

They walk over to Mac and shake hands. Mac says, "Glad to have you both. We mapped the fires, and we jotted some points of interest on the board to get us started. Please add anything you can."

Both guys contribute to the case file. Ideas about where to start in the investigation and the next fires' locations bounce around the table. Everyone agrees they need to examine the scenes firsthand and speak with the owners. Time is of the essence, so they plan to leave in the morning. They decide to drive together so they can talk along the way.

As they prepare to leave for the day, Tyrone walks into the conference room. Mac introduces him to the ATF guys, and Bradley acknowledges they have worked together in the past. Bradley and Tyrone spend a few minutes catching up on the job and their families. Before leaving for the day, Tyrone receives updates, and he receives an invitation to travel with the others, which he accepts.

Mac and Spencer leave the office and go to her parent's house for dinner. She visits them before she embarks on a trip if time allows. Her father, Myles, has been away on a business trip, and she has not seen him since his return over two weeks ago.

"Mac, how do you feel about working with ATF?" Spencer glances at her, waiting for a reply.

"Why do you ask? I have never worked with them before. José and Bradley seem to know the job, and they offered some fresh ideas today. Give me a few days with them, then ask me." During the drive, Mac wonders why Spencer asked her about the ATF guys, since they've been partners from the beginning of her career.

Mac's parents greet them at the door with hugs. Mac shares their case with her dad. Myles gives Mac his file on his company's investigation into Hunter Bows. Now that Hunter is dead, the file means nothing to his company. Mac and Spencer read the file but find nothing helpful. It just reiterates what they already know about Hunter. The police never proved wrongdoing by Hunter Bows.

On the drive to Spencer's house, Mac asks, "Do you find it odd we haven't received notice of another fire? Based on the arsonist's prior timetable, he's due to set another one."

"It is odd. I had the same thought while sitting at the dinner table with your parents. Maybe he's satisfied his urges." Spencer's phone chimes with an incoming text message. He glances at it, then turns the screen dark.

Mac watches his movements, unsure whether to mention them. "You don't believe that any more than I do. There will be more fires. The only questions are when and where."

Chapter 6

Mac's alarm blares until it falls to the floor next to the bedside table. Once she is coherent, she remembers the trip. She packed her bags last night, so all she needs to do is shower and dress. Being a woman in a man's world, she tries to stay a step ahead by being on time or early for an event. She doesn't want to break her rhythm now.

The team meets at the office, and at eight o'clock, their black Suburban, loaded with agents and gear, turns left out of the FBI field office parking lot. The agents' first stop is Knoxville, Tennessee, to meet Rob and Sally Olson, the owners of a burned gun store and home.

Spencer starts the conversation. "Did anyone learn anything new late yesterday afternoon?"

Tyrone speaks up. "A Molotov cocktail sparked all the gun store fires. The house fires are still undetermined. The ash test from our lab should be in today. I've never experienced a fire that I couldn't pinpoint the cause. I'm eager to hear from them." Tyrone looks over at Bradley, who shrugs his shoulders. He can't answer for their lab or what started the house fires, either. No one can.

Mac questions Tyrone. The unknown cause of the fire intrigues her. "What can cause a house to burn that would be undetectable to you? That seems unusual."

"It is unusual. I have focused my career on fire detection and explosives. After decades in the business, I thought I had seen it all, but obviously,

I'm wrong. In the past few days, I've researched the same question you asked me. Certain chemicals are hard to detect, but I can't imagine our guy having access to something like that. I'm still at a loss for this." Tyrone shakes his head in frustration. "While the stores burned with a Molotov, all the house fires started with something different. Something that leaves no trace, so far."

José jumps into the mix. "Tyrone, could the guy have used a Molotov, but instead of throwing it, maybe he placed it in a trash can?"

"He could have, but he didn't. There were no traces of gasoline at the origin of the house fires. Gasoline was the expected accelerant since they used it at the store fires. However, it surprised us when we didn't find it. There were no visual signs of anything used to start a fire. I've spoken with the fire investigators handling the out-of-state fires, and their house fires are like Atlanta. They have no visual evidence to explain the house fires either. Knoxville and Lexington sent their evidence for an ash test a few days ago. Cincinnati sent theirs yesterday. Atlanta's results will interest us today. If all the house fire tests match, that will be amazing."

The group sits back and wonders what caused the homes to burn and who is doing this. No one has an answer yet. They hope the owners have some information to share, but if they are like Hunter Bows, everyone loves them and their business.

Knoxville, Tennessee, is a lovely city. The sun is shining brightly when they enter the FBI field office parking lot. Williams called ahead to the office and arranged a conference room for the group to meet with Rob and Sally Olson. The agents have just enough time to freshen up before the meeting begins.

The Olson's are prompt, and an agent escorts them into a first-floor conference room of the office building. Mac offers water or coffee, but they decline both.

Spencer asks several questions of the couple. They are married with two grown children, and neither Olson has received any threats from upset customers. The police surprised Mr. Olson when they notified him of the gun store fire. His insurance policy is active, but it will not cover everything in the store. Mrs. Olson states she doesn't want the police thinking they started the fire so they could receive insurance money. If they can't collect on the insurance policy, they will have lost everything they have worked for over the past thirty years. Besides, she would have never burned her home. All her sentimental treasures were in that house, including their family pictures, and their antique furniture suffered fire damage.

Bradley asks the Olson's if either of them knew the other gun store owners. He laid a photo of each owner with their name printed on the bottom along the middle of the table. The Olson's said no, they do not know the other owners.

Each agent takes part in questioning the Olson's, but there is nothing of importance discovered in the end. The Olson's are honest, hard-working people. They own a gun store close to the interstate. The team releases the couple after they exhaust all questions.

After the meeting, the agents climb into the Suburban and drive to the crime scene. Crime scene tape blows in the breeze as they walk toward the burned-out shell of the gun store. A local deputy meets the group, permitting entrance to the premises.

Tyrone prepares to enter first. He wears gloves and booties by the time the introductions conclude. Multiple plastic baggies stick out of his backpack. With a clipboard in one hand and a handheld digital reader in the other, Tyrone is all business and eager to see the remains.

Mac enters the darkened building and does her own snooping. Each agent walks off in a different direction as flashlights flitter across the building's shell in search of evidence. Tyrone instructs the agents that if they find anything questionable, he needs to see it. They scour the burned shell of the gun store for over two hours. Tyrone carries bags of ash out to the truck. He catalogs them while waiting for the rest of the group to gather.

José marks an area inside the gun store for Tyrone to investigate. He describes it as a hole in the floor. Tyrone looks at José with an odd expression. "Show me the way."

The group follows José back into the store, and he points at a hole in the floor on the right side of the building toward the rear. "What do you make of that hole? I didn't find another like it."

Tyrone looks all around and above them. As he looks at the ceiling, it makes sense. "José, this is where one of the Molotov's landed after it burned through the roof. You have a trained eye. Maybe you should think about changing careers." Tyrone gives José a fist bump for the find.

"No way, man. I like it right where I am." José waves off the compliment and marches back to the truck. On his way, he asks, "Hey, Tyrone, what all do you have in the baggies?"

"I collect my ash samples when I investigate crime scenes using the grid method. It is something I learned a long time ago. My guess is when the lab separates the residue from the ash inside these bags, they'll find they match Atlanta, and I can testify to the grid pattern of collection. I have no explanation for the house fires, though. There have been no ignitable liquid residues in any of the tests."

"Ok, guys. It's late, and we haven't eaten all day. How about we grab supper, then we can get a good night's rest and start early for Lexington? Our meeting with Henry and Harriet O'Brien is at ten in the morning," Mac suggests as she listens to her stomach growl.

"I am hungry and tired, too. So, I agree with Mac," states Bradley. With that, the group loads up the Suburban, finds a restaurant, and enjoys a quiet supper at a steak house. They discuss the case, adding new ideas. Some scenarios sound wild, but some are possible. Mac adds the ideas to her cards for later. In a case with so little evidence, anything is possible.

Williams calls Spencer's cell phone just as the group exits the restaurant. "Hi, Williams. We are leaving a restaurant. Give us a second to get into the vehicle. Then, you will have us all on the call." Thirty seconds later, Spencer places his cell phone in the console, and the vehicle's Bluetooth connects.

For the next fifteen minutes, Agent Williams hears updates on the status of the investigation. The lack of evidence disappoints Williams, but he doesn't elaborate. Instead, he advises the group they have no new fires to report, and the call ends.

With eyebrows raised and eyes wide, Spencer and Mac exchange a look. The conversation with Williams was short on words, and he is never short on words.

Thirty minutes later, the agents are inside their hotel rooms, preparing for sleep. Mac, on the other hand, updates her note cards. She keeps her personal case book with her, but her book differs from most. Mac makes use of index cards by adding important features of the crimes and persons of interest. The cards make an excellent reference while traveling. Although it takes time to catch up, she is more relaxed as she lays her head on the pillow, knowing she is back on track with her case file. However, her mind runs in a million different directions between the case, Spencer's mysterious phone calls, and Agent Williams, who must have personal issues because he never cuts a conversation short. If anything, he adds to it.

The group's night is quiet. They review case notes and ideas, just waiting for something to lead them in a certain direction. The team knows they can't follow this firebug across the country for long. But while they have a break, they sleep.

Traffic at six-thirty in the morning is horrible. The group suffers through stop-and-go traffic for over an hour before it breaks loose. Henry and Harriett O'Brien are waiting for the group when they arrive. Mac swears to herself as they hurry into the FBI field office. She despises being late.

Henry and Harriett sit side by side at the table in a bland room. The couple stares at opposite walls. They do not look at or speak to each other, nor do they hold hands, as the Olson's did. Body language says a lot in an interrogation. It surprises Mac, as it does Spencer.

As usual, Spencer starts the questioning. Henry does the talking, and he never looks at his wife as he answers. The torched store, along with several adjoining stores, was beyond repair. Henry admits to carrying an insurance policy on the store, so nothing unusual so far. Mac takes over with Harriett, asking about the home. Harriett informs the agents that the back wall of the garage was the only damage. They got lucky with the weather because a sudden downpour helped extinguish the flames before they spread.

José and Bradley watch the exchange between the couple. It baffles both men that the husband and wife do not share a glance with each other. José gives up and asks the couple point-blank, "Mr. and Mrs. O'Brien, can you share with us why you refuse to look at each other? What's going on?"

Harriett's unshed tears pour down her face, and Henry's face turns bright red. Bradley passes a tissue box to Harriett while they wait for her to compose herself. She looks at her husband. "Well, aren't you going to tell them?"

"Tell us what? Henry, what do you know?" Bradley asks in a terse tone.

Henry clears his throat. "I knew Hunter Bows. We met at a gun show in Atlanta many years ago. Until a year ago, we were casual acquaintances more than anything. Hunter shows up at my gun store out of the blue. He acted like he was heading on a trip somewhere and just stopped by to say hello. Hunter asked me to accept a gun order for a friend of his that lived up north. The friend would pick the gun up on their way home. I wouldn't even have to collect any money. Hunter would handle that part of the deal. Over the year, this occurred three or four times until I started asking Hunter questions. Then he got testy with me. Harriett told me to stop accepting the packages, but I couldn't find the words to tell Hunter. Then all of this happened. Harriett is angry at me. At least the house didn't burn down." Henry's shoulders sag, and he releases the breath he has been holding, having kept this secret for so long. Once he makes his statement, Mac watches as his body deflates like a balloon losing its air.

Henry reaches over, grabs Harriett's hand, and asks for her forgiveness right in front of four agents. The men turn away while Mac watches the re-emergence of love, a love that had been around for decades. Now, the couple can repair their relationship, and the agents can concentrate on the packages received by Henry O'Brien. A tingle of excitement works its way up Mac's spine.

Chapter 7

After the couple leaves the office, the agents regroup and decide on their plan of attack. Two components require attention: the packages and the crime scene. Bradley and José take the packages and the remaining three heads to the crime scene. Mac, Spencer, and Tyrone agree to stop at the gun store first, then head over to the O'Briens' home.

Bradley and José pull up chairs to their laptops. José keys the instructions in the computer program, and they wait for Hunter's records to load. Both guys dread the paperwork they will have to peruse over the next several hours. Mr. O'Brien agrees to email over his files by as soon as he returns home. The ATF agents will compare Hunter's records to Henry's. Their hope is something pops up sooner rather than later. It would allow them the chance to investigate the lead instead of sitting behind a desk.

Tyrone talks about the arsonist as soon as the truck is in reverse. "You know, guys, the number of fire cases we are investigating classifies the perpetrator as a serial arsonist. The serial ones are the most serious, too. You can't tell when or where they will strike again. Everything about the arsonist becomes unpredictable. Some, once they satisfy their urges, drop off the face of the earth, escaping capture. This arsonist, though, I feel, is acting on revenge, and if he is, his job is not complete."

"That is some serious talk, Tyrone. If you think this is revenge, why isn't he done? How long do revenge arsonists keep going?" Mac asks while glancing back at Tyrone.

"Most revenge arsonists never find an acceptable end. Now, they might get arrested on another charge and sentenced to jail, thus leaving the police chasing a cold trail. However, some arsonists take months or even years off from the fire-setting. Then, for some weird reason, they pick it up again."

This time Spencer jumps in. "Are we wasting our time making this trip? Should we have stayed in Atlanta and worked it from there? Is that the starting place?"

"It most definitely was the starting place, at least in my opinion. My captain didn't share with me if there had been other fires in Georgia or elsewhere until these three popped up on someone's radar." Tyrone explains.

The thought of wasting time drives Mac nuts. "I want to check out Carter Pike and then get back to Atlanta. If Tyrone is correct, we need to be in Atlanta. If it started with Hunter Bows, we need to trace his last week on earth, who he spoke with, where he went, his spending, all of it. Hunter is the source of this chaos, and we need to know why."

Tyrone agrees with Mac, nodding his head. While Spencer drives, Tyrone writes notes in his book and checks his email for the ash reports. He doesn't understand why it is taking so long. He fires off another email, asking for the results, and lays his head back with a sigh.

Rain pours in Cincinnati when the Suburban pulls to a stop in a hotel parking lot. The trip took longer than expected because of the stormy weather. Tyrone calls Bradley and advises him of the situation. Bradley and José will get a room in Lexington while the other three stay in Cincinnati for the night. Mac calls Williams with an update, and he states FBI Agent Notting will meet them in the morning, and escort them to the gun store and the Pike residence.

The three enjoy dinner and then crash into bed for some much-needed sleep, except Mac. At midnight, Mac is still wide awake writing note cards. She can't shake the comments Tyrone made about the arsonist. She jots questions in her notebook. What type of trigger would it take for someone to set fires, especially those that kill innocent people? Why the lag in between fires? Is it job-related or personal? Is the arsonist searching for his next target during the delays? Mac knows her body requires sleep, but her mind won't stop. Two hours later, she collapses in bed and falls into a fitful sleep dreaming of Spencer, fires, and phone calls.

The next morning brings Mac a headache. Her brain has too much going on inside of it to allow her to rest. She walks into the breakfast area of the hotel and picks up a bagel and a large coffee. As she sits down at the table with Spencer and Tyrone, Spencer asks, "Not a lot of sleep, huh? Or not enough makeup?" Tyrone chokes on his coffee when he hears Spencer's question. He looks at Mac and shakes his head from side to side to calm Mac.

Mac glares at Spencer, and he realizes his comments were hurtful and immediately apologizes. Besides, he doesn't want to endure Mac's wrath all day, especially as her eyes have dark circles under them this morning.

"No, to answer your question, I slept little last night. I couldn't stop thinking about this case. Can we please eat and get on the road? The sooner we look around at the store and the house, the sooner we can head home. I agree with Tyrone that we are wasting time looking at this stuff. The only useful information we picked up was the connection between Henry and Hunter. If Hunter covered his trail, nothing would pan out from that either."

Tyrone agrees, "I'm with you, Mac. Let's get the show on the road." He knew he needed to step in and bust up this twosome before someone says something they will regret later.

Spencer keeps his mouth closed. He follows Mac's lead by eating breakfast and gathering his things for checkout. Once in the vehicle, he settles down a bit. "Our escort this morning is Agent Notting. Let him know if there is anything in particular you want to see or ask." Neither Mac nor Tyrone responds. Their noses are in their case files, while Spencer considers his earlier statement. Maybe he shouldn't have mentioned Mac's eyes.

Arrival at the FBI field office is non-eventful. The clouds appear to be holding buckets of rain just like yesterday, but the roads are dry so far. Agent Notting meets the trio at the reception desk. After introductions, the group hits the streets.

Notting suggests viewing the gun store first in case the rain starts.

Another black Suburban greets them in the parking lot. Notting brings up the fire, and Tyrone handles the conversation. Tyrone explains about the Molotov and the ash test. While the cause for the house fires is still unknown, the ash test will provide the needed information.

Most of the gun store burned to the ground, with only the back left corner standing. Agent Notting states Pike ran a gun range in the back, which consisted of twenty bays, each twenty-five yards long. There were soundproofing and vents for the lead exposure. The store and range were active. Carter's business hours had him staying later some nights to accommodate the working people. The police have no reports of any complaints about Carter Pike or the store. The police detective and the FBI are both baffled who would target Carter Pike.

"That's what we are trying to determine. Something ties these owners together, but we don't know what that is just yet." Mac explains as she continues, "Are you familiar with the name Hunter Bows?"

Agent Notting's eyebrows bunched together. "The name sounds familiar, but it might be because of this case. I can investigate it when we get back to the office. How is he related?"

"His store and home were the first to go. The house fire took the lives of Hunter and his wife, Caroline. We also discovered later somebody purchased a gun used in an Atlanta drive-by shooting at his store. The gun's owner reported it stolen a year ago."

"Interesting information, Mac. Do you think there is a correlation between the drive-by and the fires?" inquires Notting as he sees a connection.

Spencer jumps into the conversation. "We met with the alleged shooter, and we know he didn't do it. Mac and I think this kid is protecting someone. The kid says he was a passenger in the car, not the driver. The driver was the shooter. We left our cards with him, hoping he will call and give up the driver."

"Until the kid calls, you got zip. I know how that goes all too well. Here is the store. Walk around until your heart's content. I will be out front. I don't want the media thinking they can join the party because once they notice a car, they gravitate to the area for comments." He drops the threesome at the door and parks in a spot at the front. Agent Notting walks to the back of his vehicle and leans on it while giving the surrounding area a good inspection.

Tyrone, Mac, and Spencer dress in booties and masks again. This dress code is becoming way too familiar. The group steps through charred debris, and Tyrone immediately finds melted pieces of plastic jugs, confirming the same type of Molotov torched the store. Everything Tyrone sees confirms the same arsonist started all the store fires, but why? What brings the perpetrator this far away from Atlanta?

The trio inspect every inch of the store. They find no other evidence, so they make their way to Carter Pike's home. The sky grows darker than when they began. With luck, they will inspect the house and be on the road before the weather hits. Agent Notting is on the phone when they climb into the truck.

Ten minutes later, they turn into the driveway of Carter's burned house. The house sits in a cul-de-sac on a large lot in the back of a neighborhood. It is an older house, but well maintained. It is a Cape Cod style with a two-car attached garage. A workshop sits in the fenced backyard surrounded by trees. Mac glances around when they exit the truck and spots plenty of places for the fire-setter to watch this house. The vegetation is mature and provides ample coverage for someone to hide. Mac wonders where the arsonist hid. Did he choose behind the workshop, the oak tree, or the woodpile? He had so many choices that any would work.

Mac looks at Tyrone and Spencer, and they noticed the same. They proceeded into the remnants of the house. Tyrone goes straight to the back of the garage wall and confirms the style matches with the others. No melted plastic jug pieces on the scene. Whatever ignited this fire, it started on the back wall of the garage and went from there. As Tyrone looks up, he notices a neighbor peering out their window at him. "Mac, can you come over here?"

"What do you need, Tyrone? I hope you found something useful." Mac says as she maneuvers herself through the charred debris.

"See the lady in the house next door watching us from the upstairs back window of her home. How about you knock on her front door and see what she has to say about this fire?"

Mac spots the lady Tyrone refers to with a turn of her head, and she walks over to the neighbor's house. The neighbor's home is a typical two-story home with a two-car attached garage and outdoor living space. All the front windows are closed with plantation shutters. This time of the day, window blinds are usually open for the light. So, Mac grows more apprehensive as she approaches the front door.

While Mac waits to interview the neighbor, the men conclude their inspection of Carter's house. They walk to the back of the neighbor's house, looking for an advantage point. Ten steps into the backyard, they find it. It is a space between the back fence and the side of the house. Large hydrangeas grow unkempt in the fence corner, and they create the perfect hiding place.

Spencer pushes through to the back of the flowers, not sure what he expects to find. He shakes off his arms when the wetness from the flowers soaks through to the skin. "Great. Now, I am soaking wet. There's not much worse than wet clothes. The ground is soggy back here too, either from rain or a sprinkler. Now that I have walked it, we have no chance of shoe prints, but I found two broken limbs. Our guy could have very well staked out Carter's house from this location. Wait, what is this? I found something." He makes his way out of the flowers and onto the path of the guys.

"Is that a label?" Tyrone asks as he scrutinizes the white paper.

"I believe it is, or part of one, anyway. It appears torn down the middle. We still have part of a barcode, and if we trace it, it might lead us to the store and the item."

Mac waits patiently for the door to open as she hears the faint mumble of the men talking. She hears the footfalls coming down the hardwood steps toward the front door. The door pulls inwards, and an ashen lady greets Mac and introduces herself as Mrs. Isom. After she introduces herself, the lady invites Mac inside, and they sit in a parlor just inside the front door.

"What is this about, Agent Morris?" Mrs. Isom inquires while rubbing her hands together.

"We were looking into the fire at Carter's house and were wondering if you saw or heard anything that might be of help to us." Mac offers while surveying the house.

Mrs. Isom ponders the question. She doesn't want to mettle into other people's lives, but this guy was a neighbor for many years. She always felt safe knowing he was next door when her husband traveled. "I saw something I thought peculiar. It was two days before the fire when I was sitting on the back deck on the far side of the house from Carter's. I noticed a guy dressed in all black walking around the perimeter of Carters' fence. I knew the police had been watching Carter's since his gun store burned, so I just assumed this was part of the police work."

"Could you describe the guy, Mrs. Isom?"

"Not really. I didn't see his face. He had on a black sweatshirt with a hood pulled low over his head. The guy moved like a middle-aged person, but with a limp. He walked all around, and then he left through the backyard. We have a cut-through between our houses that allows us to enter the park on the next road over without having to drive around the block."

"Did you hear anything, like a vehicle, after you saw him leave?" Mac asks, trying not to rush the lady. Her nerves are firing on all cylinders. This is their first sighting of the guy, and she wants to share the news. The guy could have used the road behind them as an escape route, too.

"There was a loud rumble in the distance, but I can't say if it was coming from the park. I'm not good with sounds and distance."

"Thank you for your time, Mrs. Isom. Here is my card if you think of anything else. Please call any time, day or night."

Mrs. Isom escorts Mac to the front door and notices the guys standing at the edge of the yard, looking at something in Spencer's hand. As Mac walks over to the group, she states, "It looks like both of us came away with information."

Spencer turns to Mac. "You first. Did the lady tell us anything?"

Mac recounts Mrs. Isom's conversation. After she finishes, Tyrone states out loud to the group, "The lady thinks the guy is older. If he's older, that destroys our profile of the guy. Typically, arsonists are young people seeking fun or even revenge. Too bad she couldn't see this guy's face."

"What did you two find while I was with Mrs. Isom, and why are you wet, Spencer?" Mac asks with a puzzled expression.

Tyrone chuckles as Spencer explains his bright idea of climbing behind the flower bushes to look around. He smiles when he lifts the half-torn label in front of Mac's face.

Chapter 8

"If you found it behind the bushes, that's an odd place for a label. Do you suppose our guy watched Carter's house from behind those bushes?" Mac questions as she points.

"That's hard to tell. We'll see if Agent Notting can help with the trace on the remaining portion of the label." Spencer explains. "Here he comes now."

Agent Notting walks over to the trio. "What's going on over here? I can see you all discussing something." Notting looks at the group and waits for a reply.

Tyrone explains the label and the visual on the guy by the neighbor. Agent Notting stammers before saying, "We had a local patrol officer stop in on Mrs. Isom, and I don't remember reading any of that information in the report. Mrs. Isom must have felt more comfortable speaking with you, Mac. Let's get the label to the lab. Finding its purchase location could be crucial."

The mood is light on the return trip to Agent Notting's office. Everyone's spirits are high with the information gleaned from Mrs. Isom and the partial label unearthed by Spencer. Mac lets her mind wander on the ride. She realizes she hasn't spoken to her dad or Agent Williams in a while. Both calls were on her to-do list before leaving for Lexington to rejoin Bradley and José.

Agent Notting heads for the lab when they reach the office. Spencer signs the evidence sticker and log. The tech guy requests fifteen minutes.

Their program can trace fewer numbers than what's showing on this label. Mac, Spencer, and Tyrone pace outside the lab in the lobby. They are eager to hear the news, and they jump to attention when Agent Notting and the lab tech enter the room.

"This label belongs to a brand of milk sold in mom and pop convenience stores in Lexington, Kentucky. I will need a little more time to locate the store. If you want to start your trip back to Lexington, I'll call Agent Notting as soon as the results are available." The lab tech turns and walks back into his workspace without waiting for a reply.

Agent Notting grins. "Great job, guys. It looks like your trip was worth it. We'll keep working our end of the fire and share updates regularly. It was nice meeting you all." He lifts his hand for a handshake.

Spencer, Tyrone, and Mac shake hands with Agent Notting and thank him for his hospitality. The trio walks to their vehicle and climbs inside. Mac requests the back seat because she wants to make calls. At the start of the ride, she speaks with her dad, and then the trio updates Agent Williams on the status of the investigation by speakerphone. Mac is eager to get the results of the ash test and the store's name.

"Has anyone spoken to Bradley or José since we left them in Lexington?" Mac asks.

"I received a text from Bradley. They are holding a table for us at the restaurant, but he didn't share any information on the case." Spencer states to the group as his stomach growls. The return trip was simple without traffic. They discussed ideas about the arsonists, but nothing concrete came from it.

With her last note card complete, Mac stows her cards in her bag as the truck makes the last turn into the hotel parking lot. Since the group desperately needs a break, they will review them later and look for plausible scenarios.

Everyone stretches as they exit the vehicle. Thirst and hunger drive the group into the restaurant in silence. Spencer rubs his neck as he walked into the building.

Bradley waves at Mac as she enters the establishment first. She turns to the guys and directs them toward Bradley's table. With the guys making their way to the restaurant's back, Mac excuses herself and heads off in the other direction. She needs a minute to herself because she hasn't come to terms with Spencer's morning comment. She freshens up, then winds her way around the other tables before taking the empty chair.

Spencer thanks the ATF guys for saving a table for them. After everyone places their drink order, the updates begin. An hour later, the ATF duo knows everything the rest of the team discovered on the trip. Then Mac speaks, "What did you find out from the financials?"

José lifts an eyebrow, showing he also has interesting information to share. "To start, Hunter Bows was indeed shady. He held several shell corporations in his name with offshore accounts to match. We are still tracing the money in one offshore account as it's tied to multiple countries. We'll start on the remaining corporations next.

Hunter and Caroline could have retired and lived comfortably anywhere of their choosing." José takes a break, and Bradley continues.

"There is no known association between the gun store owners, other than Henry and Hunter. If there's an association between the gun store owners, we are not privy to the information yet. We've tagged the packages for further investigation, too. We located the purchase orders to match what Henry told us, proving he didn't lie about his involvement with Hunter." Bradley glances over at José as he looks at his phone.

After replying to a text message, José advises they have one more piece to the financials. The last offshore bank account ended in the Cayman Islands. "I wonder if Caroline knew what her husband was doing. Her name was not on any of the accounts. However, there is another name on this account, Simon Burden. We need to find this guy, and they list his address as Hunter's Atlanta business address. There is no mention of a birthdate or driver's license number for Simon either. If we can find him, he should be able to help us with the information on Hunter's bank accounts."

"Has Simon's name shown up on any other documents before now?" Spencer questions.

José shakes his head as he replies, "Not in anything I've read."

"Ditto." Bradley adds.

Mac reiterates what they need to do over the next few days. "Our goal now is to find Simon Burden, follow up on the ash test and the label. Is there anything else?"

Spencer has an idea. "I have something. No one has mentioned this yet, so I am not sure where we stand on it. We have not checked security footage from each gun store. Maybe we can get lucky and spot the guy torching the stores."

This time Tyrone reacts. "I requested the footage for each store. The Atlanta Police are handling the request for the Bows' fire. A video should be in my email now. What I don't have is the video for the fires in Knoxville, Cincinnati, and Lexington."

Bradley agrees to handle the video request for the latest fires as Mac adds one more item to the list.

They consume their meal in silence. Occasionally, the group makes eye contact across the table, but no one speaks. The food tastes delicious, and no one wants to break their rhythm. As the last fork finds a spot on the table, Tyrone's phone chirps with a message. He shrugs his shoulders as he retrieves it from his pocket.

"The ash test results are back. However, the guy is asking for a call. Typically, he sends the results to my email. I'll step outside to place the call. Do you want to wait here?" Tyrone glances around the table.

Everyone agrees to wait at the table. The group talks about the case. Great minds work in tandem, and each person at the table works the case from different angles.

After several minutes, Tyrone returns to the table with a puzzled look on his face. "I can't tell if that is a good look or a bad look," Mac states as she watches Tyrone make his way to the table.

"Well, that was an interesting call. Are you ready for the results of the ash test? I'm glad you are sitting down." Tyrone takes his seat across from Mac and Spencer and grins.

José can't stand the wait. "Out with it, Tyrone."

Chapter 9

"Fritos."

"Excuse me?" Spencer questions Tyrone's statement.

"That was my reaction, too. The fire at the Bows' residence began with bags of Fritos. I've heard of potato chips used, but never Fritos. At least that explains why the origin was difficult to locate. There was nothing left of the accelerant. Fritos are greasy, and if bags are stacked together, along with an ignition point, you have one big fireball."

Bradley pipes up, "Well, well! That must rank at the top of anyone's list of fire-starters. So, who knows Fritos can cause massive fires? Do we have a serial arsonist recently released from prison with that MO? We can search our database for a firebug using Fritos. The list should be short."

"Since the rash of fires started in Atlanta, it's probable a prisoner recently released from a Georgia prison picked up his old ways again. I'll call our ATF partners and find out those recently released before the Bows' fire." José advises the group as he touches his contact list on his phone. He steps away while speaking with a peer. On his return, he gives us a thumbs up, "We will have the list before too long."

Mac doodles on a napkin while she ponders the latest information that bags of Fritos started a fire. That was indeed a bit of unexpected information. She jots down the names of the towns the fires have been in, and then she adds the gun store owners' names to the list. While still doodling, she says, "I don't think it's a repeat offender. This is a newbie. Why would the person target gun stores and the store's owners? There is no correlation there. Even the locations of the fires are in different states."

Spencer pauses before he states, "I don't know, Mac, José might be on to something. We should investigate all avenues, and that is one we haven't considered. We don't have any other leads to work right now unless Tyrone received the video in his email. Have you checked your email, Tyrone?"

"No, I haven't checked on the video since I received the Fritos news. I've been a little distracted. Let me look at my email." Tyrone taps the email icon on his phone. Then says "It's here. And he attached the video. We will go back to the hotel and look at it on the laptop."

"Great. Everyone grab your check and pay on the way out. We'll meet in Tyrone's room in twenty minutes." Spencer instructs the group. "I think we might be onto something between the video and the newly released prisoners." Spencer stops short when he looks at Mac's face. It's obvious she disagrees.

Once they enter the hotel, each team member goes to their room. Mac doesn't speak to Spencer as she enters hers. Her mind speeds at 100 mph with thoughts on this case. When Spencer agrees with the other members of the team, it confuses her. Spencer always backs the FBI until they exhaust all leads before he steps in with agreement. Mac can't figure out what is going on with Spencer's phone calls, and now he agrees with ATF over his own partner. Spencer didn't ask her to explain her position. The team is moving in the wrong direction, and she doesn't like to waste time. The gun stores tie together somehow, either with an illegal purchase or someone trying their best to slow gun sales. They have not found the link yet. Where is that article her dad gave her on the drive-by shooting? As she reaches for the envelope holding the story, her phone rings.

"Hi, Williams, what's up?" Mac answers as she sees the caller ID.

Agent Williams gives Mac information on the latest fire. It occurred two nights ago, but no one notified him until today. He wants the team on the road to Florida. With nighttime approaching, he suggests driving in shifts. He asks for an update on their investigation, too.

"Ok. We just made it back from supper. The team will meet in Tyrone's room in ten minutes to watch a shopping center video where Hunter Bows store is located. I'll let them know, and we'll leave for Ocala. Send everything you have on the fire. Is the owner's residence a target?"

Williams describes the owner's condition, and Mac continues, "With luck, the owner will survive. We'll question him first thing in the morning if he is able. Talk soon." Mac ends the call in disbelief. This arsonist will not let up. Every three to five days, he torches another store or home. With her notes in hand, Mac walks to Tyrone's room and knocks.

The team gathers around the small round table by the window. Everyone wants to see this video. Mac clears her throat, and the guys look her way. With their attention now on her, she shares Agent Williams's phone call. When she tells the group the owner burned in the blaze, she watches their shoulders droop. Everyone needs sleep, but they know it is not happening tonight. They agree to take turns napping on the way to Florida.

Tyrone allows Mac to finish before asking, "The video is only fifteen minutes of data. Do you think we can watch it before we leave? We can discuss it on the road trip."

The group agrees. Perched on the bed's edge, Mac watches a video of blackness. There's only one streetlight in the parking lot, illuminating only a small portion of the screen. "Not sure what you guys can see, but so far, I've got nothing," Mac states, hoping to move the show along. She wants to be in Florida right now.

Spencer points to a shadow at the bottom of the screen a few minutes after Mac's attempt to stop the video. "Did you see that? Can you rewind this thing?"

Tyrone stops and moves the line at the bottom of the video a little to the left. Twenty seconds later, the image reappears. "There, there it is, Spencer. I see it. It doesn't look like there would be enough to go on, but I say we send the clip to the IT peeps and let them take a crack at it."

"Good idea," states Spencer. "Freshen up and meet in the parking lot in fifteen minutes for the trip south."

With the city lights shining in their rearview mirror, the team hits the interstate southbound for Florida. The weather is on their side this time. Each one takes part in the driving so everyone can nap before their stop.

The group arrives in Ocala in the early morning hours. Agent Williams arranges for an agent to meet them at the entrance of the Ocala Medical Center. Spencer exits the truck first and stands next to Agent Kimball, who is petite, blond, and shapely. Mac's introduction is first, then the rest of the team follows. Mac watches Spencer and Agent Kimball on the walk to the gun store owner's room. Leif Anderson is the owner, and he's in the burn unit with second and third-degree burns over forty percent of his body. Agent Kimball warns us of Mr. Anderson's cognitive state since he is under heavy pain medication.

Spencer stands in the hallway discussing things with Agent Kimball as Mac, without hesitation, walks into the victim's room. Mr. Anderson's appearance doesn't shock Mac. She walks right up to his bedside, and his eyes watch her every move. "Hi, Mr. Anderson, FBI Agent Mac Morris, and I'm here with a team of agents investigating your gun store fire. Do you feel like answering questions?"

Leif Anderson is a well-built man with sandy blonde hair and soft blue eyes. He shifts in the bed as much as possible, as his shoulders seem to reach each side of the bed. When he settles, he answers in a weak voice. "I'll try."

Mac questions Leif. "Has anyone threatened you? Have you had any unruly customers?" The other team members enter the room and grab their notebooks, poised for valuable information.

Leif answers no to all questions. He can't explain why someone would do this to him or the other gun store owners. It makes little sense. He has had no upset customers that he can remember or any citizens criticizing gun rights.

José speaks up and asks if Leif has family members who will require police protection.

Leif simply says "no" without further explanation.

Tyrone then changes the subject and asks him if his shop has cameras. If so, they would like to look at them.

"I back the camera feed up to the cloud. I can give you my username and password for access." Leif has a coughing fit, and the group backs out of the room while the nurses come in and help settle him down. The nurses advise the group they will need to come back later in the day. Leif can't continue the discussion as his condition remains unstable.

As the group walks to the waiting room, Leif's condition shocks Mac. It's a miracle the guy survived the ordeal. Leif described the moments that he remembered. He heard a noise on the roof just seconds before a container exploded over his head. Leif looked toward the sound and saw a fireball headed towards him. The last thing he remembers is trying to dodge the ball of fire. He fell away from the ball, giving protection to his face.

The fireball landed close to his left side and severely burned his left leg and foot. Once the fire hit his leg, he passed out from the pain. He has several burned spots on his arm and chest, but nothing compared to his leg. Mac wants to know if the fire-starter knew the owner was inside the store working when the fire began. If he did, then he is a real sick person.

    The group reconvenes in the waiting room, trying to make sense of the situation. Agent Kimball asks Spencer a few questions about the case, but she doesn't offer any help. Since she knows little about the fires, she makes small talk with Spencer, and the case makes for an easy topic. José and Bradley watch the exchange between the two, and they glance Mac's way every so often.

    José's phone rings, so he steps off to the side to answer. He stays on the phone for a short while. "Guys, no recent parolees fit our description. One recent release is a guy that is in his seventies now, and he has been in prison for twenty years. I think we need to look elsewhere for suspects outside of parolees."

    The team acknowledges José while Tyrone and Mac continue their deep conversation off to themselves. They discuss the possibility of the fire-starter knowing Leif was working in his shop before the fire. "I can only hope he didn't know it, Mac. That takes the fires to a whole new level. I sure hope Leif calms down enough to provide us with his login to the surveillance account. His store appears more technical than the others, and that may help us."

Mac agrees with Tyrone and adds, "It's been two days since Leif's fire. Wonder how long we have until the next one?" Bradley takes a seat next to Mac.

"Hey, Mac. I just got an email with videos attached for Cincinnati and Lexington. Do we want to find a place to eat lunch and view the videos? We can check on Leif's status later today."

"Good idea, Bradley." Mac stands and shares with the rest of the group the plans for the next couple of hours. The team heads for the door, and Mac looks back at Agent Kimball. "Please call one of us if there is any change in Leif's condition. We are waiting for access to his surveillance account." Mac turns around and walks into the elevator.

Agent Kimball stands at the elevator door with her mouth agape. She can't believe they left her standing there, even though she is Leif's security detail. Agent Kimball turns and stomps off toward Leif's room and takes up her post again. As she sits outside the hospital room, she ponders being a part of a team. A team that investigates and captures criminals. So far, she works solo. She has had little luck with partners, and she doesn't know why.

Spencer leans over to Mac and asks, "Why didn't you invite Agent Kimball?"

With a glare to kill all doubt, Mac replies, "We don't need her. She offered nothing to our case, and she remains Leif's protection. She can't leave her post."

As Spencer understands the ramifications of his talking with Agent Kimball, he continues, "Mac, don't be jealous. We discussed the case. I didn't realize it bothered you."

Mac looks over at Spencer and shrugs her shoulders. Usually, when Spencer talks with another woman, it doesn't bother her, but she is unsure what to think about the recent phone calls. She is feeling insecure, and that is not like her. Mac is independent and always has been. She loves Spencer, but she can survive without him, too. Glancing his way again, she is unsure why those thoughts popped into her head. But they did. Now, she wonders if it is an omen of something to come.

The case requires her concentration right now because they have a crazy person setting fires in gun stores and torching the owners' homes without regard to life. The trigger still niggles at her.

Tyrone speaks up from the third row. "I have the remaining ash tests from Cincinnati and Lexington, so we can compare them to Atlanta. It will interest us to see if they match."

"Good call, Tyrone. Something tells me they will match. We have a Fritos-eating fire-starter driving Interstate 75." Bradley states as he rubs his neck.

"Bradley or José, have either of you received a list of parolees who could be potential arsonists?"

"I haven't checked my email in a while, not since I received the list from Atlanta Penitentiary. Have you, Bradley?"

"No, after lunch, we'll follow up on the parolees from Jackson State Prison, since Atlanta provided none. I'm starving." Bradley suggests.

"You know we haven't been to the crime scene. We need to visit Leif's store before nightfall." Spencer points out the team's negligence.

"How did we skip the store? It is high on the list of to-dos in any criminal investigation. Our new plan is to eat first, then visit Leif's store. Once that is complete, we will check the videos." Mac states.

After a quick bite, the team pulls up to the burned gun store. It was a free-standing building, but it sits next to a small strip center. Both buildings are a total loss. The gun store is nothing more than rubble, while the strip center's front wall still stands. The team covers their footwear in booties and slides gloves on their hands in silence as they prepare to tramp through another torched building. By now, they know how Tyrone works. He makes his grid and starts his methodical investigation. The rest of the group does their own snooping.

Ninety minutes later, Tyrone speaks. "There is nothing extraordinary here. I found some pieces of melted plastic, just like the other fires. The area where Leif was lying when the fire department found him is visible. That is where we found the melted plastic, along with bodily fluids and EMS waste. The victim is correct in his summation of the incident. I also bagged ash from that same area. Something tells me it will match the rest."

They shed their booties and gloves and place them in a sealed evidence bag. The team enters the vehicle and sighs. Spencer sits behind the wheel of the truck. "Back to the hospital, right?"

Everyone nods their heads in unison. It's obvious the team is tired and frustrated. "While at the hospital, we will view the videos in Tyrone's email. Then, one of us needs to check on Leif and see if he is up to more questions. More pointedly, can he give us the login information for his surveillance camera? I feel that might be promising for us." Spencer explains.

Mac responds, "I'll speak with Leif's nurse to get clearance." After Mac answers Spencer, all is quiet, with the agents lost in thought. Mac works through scenarios, but nothing seems to fit. She wonders how someone can travel the interstate starting fires without regard to life, and why? What makes someone start fires? The idea forms in her head that the trigger for the melee is in Atlanta. Mac remembers Willie, the kid in jail, has not called her either. Why?

"Spencer, have you heard from Willie? He hasn't called me, and I thought he would have made contact by now?"

There is silence, and Mac thinks Spencer did not hear her. Just as she taps Spencer on the shoulder, he states, "No, I haven't heard from him, and I expected his call long before now, too."

Mac jots a note in her book. They need to verify Willie is still in jail. There's a possibility he made bail, and if he did, he doesn't need to identify the driver. Another visit to the prison might prove helpful. It might scare Willie to reach out. People handle jail differently.

Once the team enters the hospital, Mac trails off to find the nurse while the rest of the team moves to the waiting room. Leif's nurse stands next to the counter, writing on a whiteboard when Mac walks up to her, "Hi, I'm FBI agent Mac Morris. We were here earlier for Leif, the man burned in the gun store."

"Yes, Ma'am. I remember. How can I help you?" asks the nurse.

"Is it possible to speak with Leif again? We had an additional question we inquired of him earlier, but his coughing incident forced us out of his room." Mac explains.

"He is in debridement treatment, which takes two to three hours. He has been away for forty-five minutes. I will let him know you are waiting for him when he returns to his room. Will you be in the waiting room?"

Mac replies, "Yes, I'll be in the waiting room. Thanks." As Mac leaves the counter, she remembers a question she meant to ask José and Bradley. They did not update the group on the packages between Hunter and Henry.

The hospital is quiet. Maybe it will continue so they can view the videos by the time Leif returns to his room. The waiting room is now the office of the FBI. Mac giggles when she sees how the guys set up shop. They push tables together in the middle of the room and place papers and laptops on the makeshift conference table.

José greets Mac at her entrance. "Any luck with Leif?"

"We are holding on to him. He is in a debridement treatment for another ninety minutes. Are we ready for the videos?"

Tyrone gestures for Mac to take a seat next to him. Mac sees a strange look in his eyes. And she doesn't want to question him in front of the group. "Yes, we are ready. This one is the Atlanta video again, and then we will move to Cincinnati and Lexington. The Knoxville video hasn't made it to us yet."

Videos play in the room for forty-five minutes. The team takes note and views different sections twice. The shadow on the Hunter Bows' video is a close match to a shot of a man wearing all black. His face isn't visible, only the back of his head and body. His clothes are not identifiable, either. They are dark-colored, could be black, green, or navy. It appears the fire-starter is between 6' and 6'3" and Caucasian. The man didn't wear gloves while he covered everything else. Why would the arsonist leave his hands uncovered? Is that a message?

Chapter 10

Mac sits in the waiting room's corner, writing notes when Leif's nurse enters the room. "Agent Morris, Leif is requesting to see you. Can you come with me while he is still awake? Debridement is so painful. Most patients collapse after treatment."

"Sure, let's go." Mac stands, and Spencer follows, asking the nurse if he can visit him too.

Spencer and Mac follow the nurse down the hall to Leif's room. Much to their surprise, he is sitting up in his bed, drinking coffee. "We didn't expect to see you so awake after your treatment. Thanks for seeing us."

Placing his coffee cup on the table, he says, "There is nothing fun about debridement. It hurts like nothing I've ever experienced before. That is where the coffee comes in to save me from falling asleep. I wrote the information you'll need to access my account. I'll give you forty-eight hours of access, and then I'm changing the password. If you need longer, let me know. I want to help get this creep off the streets. If you can think of anything else you need, you know where I am. My cell phone is on the paper, too."

"Leif, we'll capture this guy. We now have valuable evidence linking all gun store fires together. The residences remain questionable because of the way the fire started. But there is no doubt it connects the gun stores," Mac explains.

"Is that something you can tell me? What caused the house fires?" Leif asks.

Spencer stammers and then divulges the fires started with bags of Fritos. He explains how the firebug uses the Fritos to ignite the fire and how it provides ample time for him to leave the scene before the fire spreads. Fritos also leaves no accelerant residue.

The news astonishes Leif. He has never heard of anything like that before. Then his eyebrows bunch upon his forehead, and his head tilts.

"What is it, Leif? Are you okay? Want me to get your nurse?" Mac asks.

"No. Everything is fine. But I remember a guy coming into the store eating Fritos and drinking a Coke. It was the biggest bag of Fritos I've ever seen, and he carried the Coke in his coat pocket. He came in a day or two before the fire. His face might be visible on the video, but I can't remember if he came up to the counter. I think I met him closer to the front door. He was a middle-aged, Caucasian guy, and he wore a cap. He asked me questions about a certain gun. Surely, he isn't the fire-starter, but the way he acted makes me wonder."

Spencer and Mac glance at each other and share a hopeful look, knowing this might be the break they need. Spencer speaks to Leif. "Thanks for this information. We'll access your security feed soon. Our team is just down the hall." Spencer is eager to leave the room and head back to the group.

Agent Kimball meets Mac and Spencer at the door to the waiting room. "Any changes on Leif or the case?"

"We just spoke with Leif, and he provided his login credentials for his surveillance account. Join us for the show. We have viewed the videos from the other fires. We spotted a few useful snippets. Leif's description of the guy eating Fritos is the most helpful. We're hopeful the guy will be on film."

"I think I'll join you if I'm not in the way." Agent Kimball replies to Spencer as she runs through options for someone to cover her post.

The threesome enters the room as the guys watch the exchange. They are waiting for the update from Leif as Tyrone breaks the silence. "Please tell us you have something. You were away longer than expected."

Mac walks over to the table and sits down. She shares Leif's description of the gun store visitor eating Fritos. Next, she produces the credentials for the video surveillance account.

"We finally have a suspect if the guy in the store is the arsonist. It would be nice to get a picture of this guy and send it off for facial recognition." Bradley shares his excitement at the recent information.

A while later, the group continues watching the video feed. It's incredible how boring a job this is until something pops. "There he is. He wears all black, even a black toboggan with every scrap of hair tucked into the cap, too. He knows the camera is there because he stands as far away from it as possible and still speaks with Leif. Crop a picture of his face, and we'll send it on to our facial recognition unit, anyway." Bradley suggests.

Mac's phone rings, and she grabs it. The group watches as her face turns pale and her lips quiver. The conversation was brief. She states, "I'm on my way," and ends the call.

Spencer knows it is serious when he sees her face. "I must leave. Dad had a heart attack and is in Augusta Medical Center. My older brother is taking my mom down. I'll join back up with you as soon as I can."

Mac gathers her things, and Spencer touches her arm. "I'm coming with you. You shouldn't go there alone. How are you getting there?"

"I'll rent a car. It will be faster and easier than flying. You need to stay here. Keep the investigation going. I'll call when I know more." Mac and Spencer share a glance as he places his hand on her arm.

Tyrone, standing on the other side of Mac, hears the conversation. "I'm going with her, Spencer. If I have to fly back, I will. At least I know she'll arrive safely. Besides, I'd like to check on Myles, too." Tyrone states as he stands behind Mac.

"You don't have to do that, Tyrone. I can make it. This investigation is important, and they need you." Mac tries to talk Tyrone into staying. She feels terrible, leaving in the middle of the investigation. She's never lost someone close to her, and this proves she is not ready.

Agent Kimball walks over to Mac and places her keys in her palm. "Take my Suburban. It's parked in the front lot. I'll walk out with you to get my things."

"No, I can't do that. I'm not sure how long I'll be away. Thank you, Agent Kimball, but I just can't." Mac stares at Agent Kimball in disbelief. After she treated Agent Kimball poorly earlier, she still offered Mac her vehicle.

"Yes, you will. The FBI owns the car, anyway. One of my colleagues will pick me up, and I'll check out a loaner. Come on, Agent Morris, family is family. Go and be with yours."

Mac doesn't know how to handle the thoughtful gesture, so she reaches out and hugs Agent Kimball, much to everyone's surprise. Glancing around the room of people, she realizes how shocked they are to witness her show of gratitude. Mac just wants to be by her Dad's side. He needs to know she is there.

"Tyrone, if you're sure you want to make the trip. I'd love the company." Mac's eyes plead for help.

"Let's go, girl." With their notes and computers in hand, they trot to the parking lot, stopping off at their Suburban first for their personal items, then over to Agent Kimball's vehicle.

"I don't know how to thank you," Mac states to Agent Kimball as she stands by the vehicle, holding her personal things.

"No need. Just be safe." Agent Kimball gives Mac and Tyrone a slight grin, then retreats inside the hospital.

Tyrone climbs in behind the wheel and sucks in a breath. "What's wrong?" Mac directs the question at her driver.

"The seat is too close to the steering wheel. I feel like I lost a knee. We are ready now. Hold on for Driving 101." Tyrone says with a smile while rubbing his knee. "By the way, you need to call Williams."

"You're right. I'll call him now." Mac takes her phone out of her bag and places a call to Williams. She explains her situation with her dad, Tyrone, and the vehicle. Agent Kimball impresses Agent Williams, too, and he appreciates Tyrone making the trip.

Mac leans her head back on the headrest. Her mind flies in a thousand directions. She has so much going through her mind she doesn't hear Tyrone ask her a question. "Can you repeat that? I didn't hear the question."

Tyrone steals a quick glance at Mac. "I said Agent Kimball isn't all bad. At first, I didn't think you liked her very much." Tyrone states with an eyebrow lifted.

"I guess I didn't treat her very well. She is nice and all, but she rubbed me the wrong way when we first met." Mac has a hard time explaining her feelings for Agent Kimball.

"Could it have something to do with Spencer? You disliked her because she took a liking to Spencer." Tyrone gives a sideways glance at Mac as he steers the vehicle.

Mac's mouth hangs open, but no words escape. Could Tyrone be right? Is that why she didn't like Agent Kimball? It sure sounds childish coming from Tyrone. Does he know about Spencer's phone calls?

"Now that I think about it, you might be right. Spencer and I have a relationship, but we have never spoken of exclusivity. If you haven't noticed, he receives calls he keeps to himself. I suppose I'm feeling a little insecure, and I dislike the feeling. So, I guess I took it out on Agent Kimball." Mac lowers her eyes as she studies her hands.

Once Mac's confession is on the table, neither she nor Tyrone speak for a while. Considering the time of day, traffic is not bad. Mac notices Tyrone's eyes always shift as he drives. He never keeps his eyes in the same direction for longer than two seconds. The man knows how to handle a vehicle, and Mac appreciates the company.

A text message alerts Mac to more information on her Dad's condition. She holds her breath as she reads it. Her biggest fear in life has always been losing her parents. She knows it will happen one day, but she is not ready for that day.

"What's the word?" asks Tyrone with concern.

"So far, so good. Dad has a heart Cath procedure in thirty minutes. He is alert and talking." Mac lets out a breath she doesn't realize she is holding.

"Sounds good to me. Your Dad is a tough old brute. He will be fine. I know you are worried, and I am too, but if he is alert and talking, he'll be fine."

Mac can't answer because of the lump in her throat. She doesn't cry often, but when it involves her parents, all walls crumble. Her cell phone remains in her hand. Just as the screen turns black, it lights up again with a message from Spencer.

Agent Notting called with an update on the label. It's from a pint of milk purchased at the J & S Convenience Store in Lexington. They are sending surveillance footage to his email. He'll call again later. Sending well wishes to Myles.

Mac reads the message to Tyrone. "Now, we have the possibility of new video footage from the convenience store. With the multiple videos, surely, we will have a photo of this guy. But, if he's not in the system, he'll be hard to identify. The arsonist has been lucky so far by not leaving us DNA."

Tyrone adds, "Every criminal makes a mistake at some point. No one is perfect. If he keeps starting fires, we'll find him. If he goes underground, we'll have a much harder task ahead of us, but it is not impossible to find him."

Sometimes sharing thoughts is difficult for Mac, but she feels she can talk to Tyrone. So she presses ahead. "My gut tells me, the trigger for this lunatic is in Atlanta. I'm not sure what the trigger is or why the person sets these fires, but it only makes sense. Agent Williams informed the pair the first fire occurred in Atlanta. They recognized no other fires with our MO. I don't want to be the one to tell the guys they are wasting their time with the list of parolees."

"I agree with you. Nothing points to anything but Atlanta. Were there any murders in Atlanta before the first fire at the store? That could be a reason. However, I'm not sure how the fire fits in with murder."

There's a pause before Mac continues. "It appears the suspect is seeking revenge on gun stores and their owners, although I can't explain why he seeks to harm the owners' residences unless he feels they are a bonus. When I visited with my parents, Dad gave me an article on a drive-by shooting that involved Hunter Bows' store."

"Whoa, what did you say? Myles knows Hunter Bows. Care to explain?" Tyrone glances at Mac as he continues to drive. His face is a mask of concern and confusion.

"I'm sorry. I haven't updated the team yet either. Yes, Dad's company provided surveillance for the ATF about two years ago. ATF was short on workforce and contracted with dad to watch Hunter 24/7 for a while. ATF suspected Hunter was transporting guns into Mexico, just as we did. Dad says he was sketchy, but they could pin nothing on him. The article was in the newspaper, so Dad kept it with his files on Hunter."

"Have you read the article yet?" Tyrone asks Mac.

"Nope. I've tried several times to sit down to look at it, but something steers me in another direction. I have it with me in my bag. We'll look at it tonight." Mac states.

The rest of the trip is quiet. Tyrone negotiates Augusta streets like a pro. He uses the FBI sign to park at the front of the emergency room entrance. Mac and Tyrone walk into the waiting room, hoping to find her family. She grabs her phone and sends a barrage of messages to her mom and brother. An answer arrives moments later.

"They moved Dad to the second floor, Room 234. Come on." Mac grabs Tyrone by the arm as a suggestion to follow.

"Why don't you go see him, and if he is up to it, I'll come in later?" Tyrone offers.

"Sure thing. But Dad will want to see you. I can promise that. There is a waiting room upstairs. Can you check in with the group in Florida, and then I'll be back to get you?"

"As soon as I get a drink, I'll call the team and Agent Williams. Take your time, Mac. Make sure all is well with Myles and your mom."

Mac walks toward her dad's room, a little apprehensive. She has never seen her dad ill, much less in a hospital bed. The door is closed when she arrives. She gently knocks on it, and her brother opens the door.

"Look who made it, Dad. It's Mac." Mac hugs her brother, Myles Jr., and he leads her into the room.

Myles, propped up in the bed, sports the biggest smile Mac has ever seen on his face. "How are you, Dad? You scared me to death." Mac walks over to his bedside, puts her hand in Myles's hand and squeezes it as she tells herself not to cry.

"I'm fine. The doctors are not sure it was a heart attack. They even canceled the heart Cath test. My vitals are normal, and I feel fine except for being a little tired. They should know if something is not right because they have me connected to every machine. How did you get here so fast?"

Mac grins as she tells her dad that Tyrone drove her here from Florida. Myles asks to see

Tyrone, as Mac knew he would. She steps out of the room to fetch him. While away, the machines in her dad's room go haywire.

Tyrone and Mac turn the corner toward her dad's room to see nurses and doctors exiting the room. Mac runs over to her mom and brother. "What happened? I was away only for a short while."

Mary, Mac's mom, speaks up. "Myles had a cardiac episode. It is the same type of event he had with George and George is the reason he is here. He made your dad come to the hospital."

"Where is George? I haven't seen him yet. Tyrone, George is dad's security leader." Mac asks as she looks down the hall.

"George is picking up where he and Myles left off. They are working on a contract in this area. George indicates everything is under control. He will be here later in the day. The doctors have reordered the heart cath. Something is causing the episodes. Tyrone, Myles wants to see you."

Mac takes Tyrone by the hand and leads him into Room 234. Myles is once again sitting up in the bed, but he looks pale and tired this time. These episodes are taking their toll on his body.

Myles's face glows when he sees Tyrone. They talk for about thirty minutes, and Tyrone excuses himself to take a call. Mac joins him in the waiting room while the nurses take Myles's vitals.

The following twenty-four hours are mixed with happiness and worry. One hour Myles is doing okay, and then he has another episode. A day after the first event, the doctor's visit and advise the family Myles will require one stent in an artery. It is a relatively simple surgery as heart surgery goes, and recovery will be minimal. He can return to regular activity within two weeks or less. Relief is visible on all. They schedule surgery for two this afternoon.

Mac and Tyrone move to the waiting room to read the article on the drive-by shooting. They read the article twice. Mac struggles, trying to understand why her dad kept this article. "I don't see how this relates to our investigation. This was a drive-by shooting on an outdoor basketball court in April. No information on the shooter or the victims."

"Think about it, Mac. Is there any information on the gun? Like where it was purchased or maybe who owned it?"

"I see nothing else here. Oh wait, here is another article. I understand now. Read this one." Mac hands the next article to Tyrone.

Tyrone reads the article in five seconds. The article is so short Mac wonders how anyone even found it in the newspaper. "Okay, so we know Hunter Bows sold the gun to someone, but then they reported it stolen, and then someone used it in a drive-by shooting at an outdoor basketball court."

Pieces fall into place for Mac. "Willie. He was with the shooter. He told us he did not pull the trigger, but the cops arrested him. I need to find out if he is still in jail." Mac grabs her phone and calls Spencer.

Spencer picks up on the second ring. "Hey, Mac. How are things in Augusta?"

"Dad will be in surgery at 2:00 this afternoon for a stent. I will know more about our schedule after the surgery is over. The doctors are optimistic. They told us this morning that Dad should be back to normal in two weeks. I'm changing the subject of our case. Tyrone and I just read two newspaper articles that Dad saved because they related to Hunter Bows. It's about a drive-by shooting, the same shooting involving Willie. Can you check and make sure Willie is still in jail? I want another crack at him. If he did not shoot the gun, he knows who did."

"I will call as soon as we finish. We should receive the surveillance footage of the J & S Convenience Store any minute. I'll text once we get it." The call ends, and Mac glances at Tyrone.

Chapter 11

"I hear a stiffness to your conversation. Try giving the guy a little leniency. You do not know who he is talking with and why. Just my thoughts on it." Tyrone pats Mac on the knee and walks to the coffee machine.

Mac shuffles through papers while she ponders Tyrone's remarks. Why doesn't Spencer share his conversations? She keeps no secrets from him. She loves Spencer, but she is unsure if she can give up her independence to anyone, not that Spencer would want to marry her anyway with their line of work. Marriage and children may never be a possibility. Her mom and dad hint about grandchildren, but she dodges the subject, hoping her brothers will pick up her slack.

Tyrone sits down with coffee and his laptop. He concentrates on responding to emails. Being on the road makes it hard to stay on top of things. A typical workday for him means his email is current before day's end. One email is of importance to the case. "Mac, the ash test from the stores confirms gasoline, and the ash test from the residences confirms the Fritos. The ATF and FBI classify the suspect as a serial arsonist. We can link him to the fires with jugs filled with gas and Fritos in his possession, if we can find him. Our case would be rock solid if we had him on video starting one fire or a witness who saw him start one."

"That's good news, I guess. At least we are not looking for multiple people. We should receive the video from the J & S store soon. Spencer is texting me when he receives it. I'm looking for a break in this case, and I hope this video is our next break."

"Nothing from the store and no results from the facial recognition in the picture from the gun store. Did José or Bradley find anything on Simon Burden?"

Mac pauses before she answers. "I haven't thought about Simon. I need to follow up on him. He must be a business partner, but no document lists him. I can't think of another reason to add a person who is not your spouse to a bank account."

With Myles's surgery looming over Mac, she spends time with him and Tyrone. The men share stories about their time in the service. Mac loves to hear stories about her dad's service time. However, her mom, Mary, does not. Mary says it was a scary time for her, and she doesn't want to know how close she came to losing Myles. While they tell stories, Mary and her sons go to the cafeteria for a bite of lunch. Milton, the youngest boy, and middle child, arrives to see Myles before they wheeled him into surgery.

The surgery begins right on time. Mac is nervous, but she tries to hide her shaking hands. Her note cards fall out of her bag, and she places them on the table and then arranges them into distinct groups. She always works them like a puzzle. "Tyrone, I'm back to my original idea. The shooting is the trigger, but it didn't happen until someone named Hunter Bows in the newspaper article. We need more information on the shooting, more than the report offers. Willie needs to divulge the driver's name. If we can find him, we can work backward. Why shoot the victims? Did the shooter know the victims? If not, who were the intended victims? I think we need to speak with the shooting survivor as he may lend some information to this whole scenario, too."

"Do we have the survivor's name anywhere? I don't remember seeing it." Tyrone asks as he sifts through mounds of paper. Then he moves to file folders in his bag and continues his search. "I don't see it in any of my notes."

"I don't either. When I speak with Spencer in a bit, I'll follow up on it. Spencer can get the information for us if it is not in his notes." Mac suggests.

George pops his head into the waiting room. "Any news on our guy?"

Mac jumps up and hugs George. "Not yet. We are waiting patiently or trying, anyway. I'm glad you made it. Dad will be happy to see you too." Mac pulls George over to where she and Tyrone are sitting. Tyrone stands as she introduces them, and they talk about Myles and how they each met him. George and Tyrone seem to strike a friendship.

Two hours later, the doctor enters the waiting room. The entire family, including Tyrone and George, are in deep thought when the doctor greets them. The doctor explains that Myles did great in surgery, and they implanted only one stent. Then the doctor states Myles will spend one night in the hospital, then they'll release him to travel home to follow up with the family doctor. The doctor speaks to Mary, advising her to locate a cardiologist near their home. With Myles' condition, his medication will require updating. After two weeks of downtime, he can return to full duty, providing he takes his medicine, and he follows up with his doctor.

Relief washes over George when the doctor confirms Myles is fine. He stands and excuses himself back to work. George shares with Mary that the job concludes in three days, and he'll stop by the house to see Myles after that. "Tell the big man not to worry about the job. We are managing without him." George hugged Mary and Mac, then shook hands with Tyrone and the boys.

"Tyrone, with dad's release tomorrow, are you okay with staying one more night?" Mac doesn't want to beg, but she really wants to be here for her dad.

"No problem for me. It is late in the day, anyway. Let's find a quiet place that we can talk on speakerphone. We'll call the group and update them. I know Spencer is eager to hear."

Fifteen minutes later, Mac and Tyrone address the group with updates on Myles and the case. José and Bradley ask Mac a few questions about her theory surrounding the shooting, and Mac returns the favor by asking about Simon Burden. José speaks up, "Without a birthday or photo on Simon, we haven't located him yet. We're working with the bank where they opened the account to secure a video of the meeting. No luck yet because you know how banks are with someone's identity."

"This guy must exist. There would be no reason to open a bank account with a fictitious name, because that could jeopardize Hunter. Simon is an actual person, or the bank would never have added his name to the account. Bank regulations are strict. Simon would have produced documents confirming his identity." Tyrone adds to the conversation.

Spencer acknowledges his team's thoughts, and he agrees. "Thanks for the updates, Mac. The video from J & S is in your email. We pulled a snippet of a photo, but we hold little hope in identification. Look at it and let me know your thoughts. We look forward to seeing you two tomorrow. Let us know what time you expect to arrive, and we'll advise Agent Kimball so she can retrieve her ride."

"We'll watch the video soon. I'll text when I have ETA. See you tomorrow." Mac ends the call and looks at Tyrone.

Tyrone guesses. "Well, Agent Kimball isn't with the group. Otherwise, they wouldn't have to notify her of our arrival time." He grins at Mac, hoping that tidbit of information would make her feel better.

Mac doesn't respond to Tyrone's comment. She gathers her things and heads back to the waiting room. Her dad should be ready to come back to his room now. Mac needs to see him before she can relax. Tyrone follows close behind.

The rest of the day and night are a blur. Both Mac and Tyrone enjoy the solitude. Mac shuffles her note cards, and Tyrone compares information from a few of his other cases. He delegates the next steps for those cases, sits back in his chair, and rubs his forehead. He feels apprehensive about this firebug. They've heard nothing over the last two days, and that makes him uneasy. Where will the next fire occur? Will the owner be a target as well? Tyrone writes himself a note to ask Leif if he remembers telling the Fritos guy if he was working at the store the night of the fire. If he did, this firebug is outrageous and undeterred by the owners' injuries or death.

They release Myles early the next morning. Once he receives notice, he states to Mac and Mary, "Take me home, please. I am ready to go."

Mac glances at her mom. "Are you okay with driving Dad home? If not, I can change plans."

Mac's oldest brother joins the conversation. "Milton and I are following them home to get Dad settled. Don't worry, Mac. Everything is fine. Go back to Florida and catch this crazy man."

"Thanks. You know I worry about everyone. Let me know when you make it home, please." Mac hugs her family as she readies to leave.

"We will, honey. Tyrone, take care of her for me. It was great meeting you. I look forward to more visits." Mary says as she pats him on the forearm.

"Yes, ma'am. I would like that." Tyrone replies as he and Myles exchange a fist bump and leaves the room. He'll meet Mac at the front of the hospital with the car. They have packed their luggage and are ready to travel back to Florida to catch up with the group.

Mac exits the hospital and sucks in a deep breath. With the blue sky overhead, nothing can take away her happiness at knowing her dad is on his way home. She spots Tyrone parked at the door and hurries to the vehicle. She climbs inside, buckles up, and then leans her head back.

Traffic in Augusta is slow around the hospital. Once they enter the interstate, they move at a steady pace. Mac texts Spencer that they are on their way to them, and Spencer responds to meet them at Agent Kimball's office.

"The gang will meet up at Agent Kimball's office. At least I can return the vehicle to her. I'll treat her nicer on this trip. She was a lifesaver letting us use her vehicle."

"She saved us a lot of time trying to rent a car." Tyrone agrees, and then he continues. "I have a question for Leif if you have a way to contact him. I want to know if he mentioned to the Fritos guy he would work late at the store the night of the fire. If he did, that might be the reason he injured Leif. He became a target. The arsonist injured the other owners as a secondary occurrence because he didn't know if they were home or not."

"That is a good question, Tyrone. I have Leif's cell phone in my bag in the back. When we stop for a break, I'll grab his phone number and send him a quick text."

After a few more miles fly by, Mac and Tyrone grow weary. Neither realized how tiring it would be to camp out in a hospital waiting room for forty-eight hours. Mac's phone signals a text. She glances at it and smiles. "Spencer sent a text reminding me the J & S video is in my email."

"Looks like we are two hours from the group, and I'm hungry. Can we grab lunch?" Mac asks Tyrone as she yawns. "We can view the video from the J&S Convenience Store, too."

"It's unlikely we'll be much help on the video, but we need to see it. On the hunger question, I can eat anytime. This exit has several eateries." Tyrone exits the highway and turns right. There is one of every fast food establishment anyone might want. Turning into a lot, they notice substantial police activity in a strip mall's parking lot behind them. Sirens blare and tires squeal as more cars pull into the lot. "Wonder what's going on, Mac?" Tyrone asks as he steps out of the vehicle, searching for the action.

"Who knows? It could be anything. Is there a gun store close by?" Mac asks as they wander toward the eatery. There are too many patrol cars to count, and their lights cast a blue glow in the sky.

"That would be odd. I didn't see a road sign for a gun store. Get down, Mac! The police are under fire!" Tyrone yells over the loud percussion of bullets ricocheting off the buildings and cars. The duo ducks behind the nearest vehicle as bullets continue whizzing past their hideout.

Police officers yell at restaurant patrons to stay inside as they exit, oblivious to the action taking place in the parking lot. The police have the alleged criminal pinned down behind a truck three vehicles away from Mac and Tyrone. Mac whispers to Tyrone, "Can we see the guy through our windows?"

Tyrone's head shakes from side to side. "No, the windows are too dark back here. Maybe if we moved to the front doors, they shouldn't be as dark. Is there is only one bad guy?"

Mac is looking under the vehicle as Tyrone asks his question. "I think so. He isn't visible under the vehicles either. He must hide by the wheel. Otherwise, I could shoot him under the cars. At least, it might slow him down for an officer to tackle him."

More shots blew past the duo, so they hid out of sight again. Time moves slowly as Mac and Tyrone wait out the interference. Mac grows more and more nervous, knowing how much this will delay their arrival in Florida. She's been away from the group longer than expected already.

A few minutes later, the gunshots subside. Neither Mac nor Tyrone can tell if the altercation has ended. Rising from the ground next to the vehicle, they search for signs it's over. They can see nothing.

Suddenly, a guy dressed in a black hoodie and black jeans comes charging toward them. Tyrone steps in front of Mac and grabs the guy by the hoodie, saving Mac from getting plowed over. "Hey, calm down, buddy. Where are you going in such a hurry?" As the guy turns to face Tyrone, he takes a gun from his back waistband and brings it up to his right side with his finger on the trigger.

Mac sees the guy's eyes widen, and she draws her sidearm and aims it at his face. "Don't try it. Put your weapon down, now." Mac fumes in an authoritative voice. The guy hesitates, considers his options, and Tyrone's face plants him on the ground, wrenching the gun away from the guy before he has time to decide his next move.

A police officer hears the commotion and runs over to the duo. He sees the guy on the ground with Mac standing over him, holding her gun. "Drop your gun and raise your hands." The officer directs his statement to Mac.

Tyrone speaks up. "We are law enforcement. My name is Tyrone Guthrie with Atlanta PD, and my ID is in my back pocket. She's my partner, FBI agent Mac Morris."

The officer pulls Tyrone's identification from his back pocket, reads it, and lowers his weapon. "Thanks, guys, for showing up in our gun battle. This creep shot one of our officers last night, and we have been searching for him all night."

Mac stands there with her mouth open, shocked at the information. "I'm glad we could help. How's the officer?" Mac questions.

"The bullet entered the lower abdomen below the vest. Lucky for him, the bullet didn't cause too much damage. He'll survive." The officer walks over to the suspect and places him under arrest by cuffing his hands together. "Do you have cards on you? I'll need your contact info for the report."

Both walk over to the Suburban and retrieve their cards. "Who picked this spot for food?" Mac asks, snickering. They pass their cards to the officer and head inside for food. Tyrone smiles.

"There is nothing like an adrenaline rush to wake you up. I'm not sleepy anymore!" He tells Mac as they stand in line for their food.

The duo enjoys a quiet lunch and then jumps back in the truck. Before pulling away from the lot, Mac opens the J&S video on her phone. While the video is short, there is only a brief glimpse of the guy purchasing the milk. The video offers a clear sight of the guy's back. With no way to identify him, Mac and Tyrone sigh. The twosome share no words.

Knowing the battle in the parking lot caused a significant delay, they still feel good because they helped catch a cop shooter. Since the video offered nothing new, Tyrone backs out of the parking space and heads for the interstate. They should have been halfway to Florida by now. Tyrone's fondness for driving relieves Mac, as it gives her extra thinking time. Minutes later, Mac's ringtone blares in the truck, and as she answers it, Spencer's tone confirms they had another fire.

Chapter 12

Tyrone also knows they're looking at another fire just by listening to Mac's voice. "Where is it, Mac?" Tyrone whispers. He watches as an exit nears. If they need to turn around, this would be the perfect opportunity.

"Spencer, send me the address. We are south of Lake City, but we still have Agent Kimball's vehicle." Mac's palms sweat as she makes sense of their situation. She takes several deep breaths to calm her body.

"Agent Kimball is here with us. She can travel with us to Lake City and then pick her truck up from there. The address is in your text messages. We're leaving now. Meet us at the fire scene. At least we can see it before nightfall."

As soon as the call ends, Mac checks her texts. She has the address and reroutes Tyrone. He takes the next exit and heads in the opposite direction. They are just over an hour south of Lake City. Tyrone is eager to see the scene. "This will be the first scene, other than Atlanta, that we are privileged to see within twenty-four hours of the fire. If we're lucky, we will find some DNA to match to the suspect." Tyrone presses the pedal a little closer to the floor. He considers turning on his lights but holds off.

Mac doesn't answer right away. A few scenarios race through her mind. Then she shares her thoughts with Tyrone. "This might sound crazy, but what if our suspect is a long-haul truck driver? The locations of the fires are still showing up close to the interstate. I can't understand why they would run with Interstate 75 unless there was a reason the suspect was on the interstate."

Tyrone smiles as he replies, "Your dad said you loved puzzle solving. A truck driver sounds very plausible to me. It would explain a lot. Have we noticed any trucks in our videos? Are you referring to pickup trucks or semi-trucks?"

"It could be either, I guess. The suspect would require money for travel and gas. Why not make money while you carry out the deed? No guarantee this is the answer, but we have no other avenue to investigate."

Mac leans her head back on the headrest and lets her mind run wild. She grabs her note cards from her bag, and her pen flies across the lines. The notecards fill with ideas and areas of interest that will require further information when she finishes.

A little while later, Tyrone turns into the parking lot of the latest fire. This fire occurred in a free-standing building facing a major road in Lake City. It is two miles from the interstate and visible from three sides, which is unusual for this suspect. Two of the four walls still stand, but the front one is the weakest. The wall creaks in the breeze, and the window blinds rattle from the draft, which create an eerie sound. The smell of burned and charred wood is nauseating.

"Dress up, Mac. I want in there as fast as I can. This is my chance to find something new and useful to identify this guy." Tyrone and Mac put on their protective clothing and walk toward the building.

"Hold up, Tyrone. My phone is ringing."
Mac answers on the third ring.

"Hey Spencer, we're at the scene and walking toward the building. If we're not in the lot by the truck, we'll be inside." Mac slides her phone into her pants pocket when the call ends and follows Tyrone into the building.

The duo flashes their credentials to the police officer on duty as they enter the burned structure. It resembles the rest of the fires, which disappoints Mac because she wants to find this guy. He's injured and killed too many people, and the suspect must pay for his crimes.

This structure boasts a unique floor plan compared to the other gun stores. There were training rooms, storage rooms, and a retail area. Some parts of the structure remain standing on the far side of the building. Tyrone places markers along his path and continues to the back of the store. His lips turn upward into a smile, but Mac looks away, instinctively knowing not to question Tyrone yet. She aims for patience and to not push him for results. Tyrone has a habit of completing his grid before sharing news, as he doesn't like interference.

While searching the farthest point in the building, Mac hears Spencer calling her name. Her pulse quickens, and she sucks in her breath. Spencer still takes her breath away. Mac realizes it excites her to see him, but it makes her mad, too. She wonders if Spencer is trying to separate from her, not sure why, but with the secretive phone conversations, what else could it be?

Spencer walks up and pecks Mac on the cheek, and says, "I missed you. I'm glad you're back." Then he squeezes her hand as he walks toward Tyrone.

A weight lifts from Mac's shoulders as she feels grateful for Spencer. "Where is the rest of the crew?" Mac asks as she looks behind Spencer, expecting them to be following.

"They are speaking with their boss. They'll be here shortly." Spencer answers over his shoulder.

Mac and Spencer walk up to Tyrone as he places something in a plastic bag. "What did you find, Tyrone?" Spencer asks.

"Hey, Spencer. I located some fibers that appear to be a match to Henry's residence fire. I found them along the rear of the yard. It might be from a jacket or shirt. If it is the same, we can place the suspect at two fires. Once we get the guy, DNA will take care of the rest."

José, Bradley, and Agent Kimball walk in the side door of the roofless building. Mac greets them and then takes Agent Kimball aside and expresses her gratitude for the use of her vehicle. After a few minutes of conversation, they join the group. Spencer requests an update from everyone, so they agree to locate a hotel for the evening and meet over dinner.

Agent Kimball heads back to Ocala but requests updates as the chase continues for the firebug. Mac agrees to send updates as they are available. If Ocala receives any new tips, she will forward them as well. The group watches and waves as she turns right out of the lot, heading to the interstate.

Tyrone closes the back of the truck after he places his finds in his crime scene box. "Are we ready to find a hotel? I am tired and need a shower. Fire smells should not bother me anymore, but I don't enjoy walking around smelling like a fire pit," he says as he scrunches up his nose.

"I agree with Tyrone. There is a hotel about a half-mile down the street to the right." Bradley states. Spencer jumps into the driver's seat, and everyone else piles in wherever they can.

After dinner, the group takes their time discussing the aspects of the case. They start from the beginning and end with the latest fire in Lake City. Mac shares information received from the on-duty police officer at their arrival. The owner of this range, Jerome Taylor, is in police protection, along with his girlfriend, Tina Englebrit. No one wants to take the chance of the fire-setter showing up at the owner's home.

"That brings up an idea," interjects Bradley. "Should we stake out the owner's home in case the arsonist drops by the house later? It would be something to catch him in the act."

Everyone looks around the table, contemplating Bradley's idea. "I like it. Should we do it tonight? It hasn't been forty-eight hours since the store burned, and he torched the other residences from two to three days afterward. Do we all agree to the stakeout tonight? If not, speak up now."

No one disagrees, so the group gathers their things and heads to their respective rooms to change into stakeout gear. Mac feels like this stakeout has a possibility of capturing this guy in the act. The fire-starter will not show up if he knows the gun range owner is in police protection. Did the police in Lake City release that information to the media? Mac shakes her head as she knows the cops will keep that information close, or at least she hopes they will.

Dressed in black, everyone meets for the trip to Jerome's. Hotel patrons weren't sure what to make of the group dressed in all black. But, with FBI, ATF, and ATL PD stitched across their backs, no one questions them as they walk to their Suburban.

The moon glows across the night sky, and every so often, light wispy clouds pass overhead. The air is not cold but a little crisp for this area, and Mac is thankful for her lightweight jacket. It is excellent for weather like this, and it also helps to conceal her weapon.

Tyrone begins the conversation. "Do we have a plan, other than a stakeout?" Who does what and when?" Tyrone looks at the guys for an answer.

Spencer takes the lead since stakeout plans are nothing new to him. He spent time on a SWAT team in his police officer days, and he was on the FBI SWAT Team. He passed on the most recent FBI SWAT callout because his heart has not been in it since the death of his commander a few months ago. A sniper shot and killed Commander Burke at his residence, and Spencer is still coming to terms with his death. Spencer knows he must decide whether to continue with the SWAT team, but he is not ready to determine that yet.

"Since there are five of us, we have plenty of coverage for the home. Once we see the home, we can decide on vantage points. We have ear comms for everyone in the back of the truck. These are strong enough to hear a whisper. If you need to speak, you can whisper without giving away your hiding spot."

Mac continues. "We need to be in place by midnight. The reports list the fires started between 1:00 and 3:00 am, which is odd since the store fires start earlier in the night. If we get close to the home and spot a motel, I want to ride through the lot and check for semi-trucks or pickups. A truck driver is the only job that explains the fires along the interstate. I can't imagine anyone living in Atlanta, driving to each of the fires, starting it, spending a couple of days to torch the owner's home, driving home, and then a few days later, doing it all over again. That would make no sense at all."

"When you explain it like that, it makes little sense. The truck driver would have a reason to be on the interstate." José admits while nodding his head.

Tyrone speaks again with a tinge of urgency. "Did someone call the Lake City police department and advise them of our stakeout? I don't want to get arrested tonight."

"I did. Also, our backup will patrol the area but not too close. We don't need a reason to spook the firebug," Spencer answers as he turns onto Mr.

Taylor's street. "This is a pleasant surprise. Hunter's home was the nicest by far, until now. How in the world does this guy live in a home like this by owning a firing range?"

Bradley cranes his neck, looking out the passenger window. "We might need additional people to stake out this house. Has anyone checked into Jerome's background? He must have other financial interests outside of guns."

No one speaks as they look at each other. Mac jots a note in her book to do just that. What if Jerome and Hunter Bows are friends? That would mean Hunter, Henry, and Jerome knew each other. Is that a pattern? "Bradley, I have a note to check into Jerome's background. We will handle it in the morning." Mac confirms.

Spencer drives slowly down the main subdivision road, glancing in all directions. It's a small cluster of homes situated off a major highway. There might be twelve homes total—all of which are huge and sit on microscopic lots. Some homes boast circular drives in the front yards with water fountains in the center, while others have palm trees lining the driveway. A few homes are brick, while the rest are stone and siding. Jerome's home is a combination of stone and brick with a massive front porch. If the arsonist starts a fire here with the houses so close, it would be catastrophic because of the neighbors' proximity.

The plan is coming together for Spencer as he continues to drive around. He locates a road behind the subdivision, and he drives down it, not sure why, but following his gut. He continues to steer away from Jerome's home. "I don't see a hotel within walking distance to Jerome's. Has anyone found one on a map? If not, I'm not sure how the firebug will handle this without the possibility of escape."

"I don't see one either, Spencer. Is that another road on the other side of the neighborhood? We need to check from that direction too for a truck and workable escape route." Tyrone suggests as he points to the road behind the neighborhood.

The truck turns right, then left as Spencer drives them to the other side. With the front of the subdivision facing a major road, it doesn't afford a parking area. There is no other road to use for concealment. As soon as Spencer turns on the street, everyone sucks in a breath. This road is perfect, with woods on both sides and a house sitting back from the road. Spencer slows the truck to take a sharp curve. When they come out of the turn, they face a pickup truck with no visible occupants parked toward the road's edge.

"Well, look what we found. Gear up for a traffic stop." Spencer instructs the group.

He pulls alongside the truck at an angle and slows to a stop. Just as the team opens the truck doors, the driver pops up behind the wheel and speeds off, spinning his tires and causing debris to fly onto the black Suburban. Spencer drops the truck into drive, completes a 180 turn, and follows the pickup truck onto the major road.

Mac grabs her cell phone and dials Lake City Police for help. She calmly speaks as she describes the truck and its location while holding onto the ceiling handle. Mac tosses about in the front seat as Spencer races behind this pickup. "Can anyone read the tag number?" Spencer asks as he concentrates on the truck in front of him.

"No. I can't. It looks like mud covers the tag." Mac answers. "Did anyone get a good visual on this guy?" Mac keeps her focus on the truck.

"All I noticed was a black stocking cap covering his hair and ears. I can tell you he is Caucasian." Then Spencer adds, "He must have been lying in the front seat, hoping no one would stop and ask questions about his parking there. I should have expected this." Spencer slaps the steering wheel, expressing his frustration.

They follow the guy for miles. The truck driver flies over railroad crossings and blows through traffic lights. Mac continues to speak with dispatch as local officers join the pursuit. They watch the truck hit a patrol car and send it into Spencer's path. Spencer maintains control as he swerves to avoid a near-fatal encounter with the officer. After their truck comes to rest on the shoulder of the road, Spencer shakes his head. "Is everyone okay?" He looks around at his passengers.

"Great driving, Spencer. I know the officer feels the same. We would have hit him in the driver's door, probably killing him, if you didn't stop. We need to check on him. I know we lost the fire-starter, but you also saved someone tonight." Tyrone says to Spencer, patting him on the shoulder as he tries to come to grips with the situation. After several deep breaths, Spencer slides out of the truck.

Mac is already out of the truck and running to the officer's side. "Are you okay?" Mac asks the officer, opening his door to see for herself.

"Yes, I think I'm okay. That was some driving by your guy—good thing he can handle vehicles. Otherwise, I would not be here. I want to shake his hand." The officer states as he limps toward Spencer.

Tyrone calls for Mac, and she walks back to him. "Dispatch is holding for you. You didn't end the call with them when you exited the vehicle."

"I jumped out of the truck to check on the officer and didn't report." Mac picks up her phone from the truck's floorboard and describes her situation with dispatch and then requests a status on the other vehicles in the chase.

A dispatcher reports the chase ended when the truck driver wrecked on a curve on a narrow side street. The driver somehow survived the accident and ran away on foot. The police called for K9 dogs and helicopters to help with the search, and the helicopter's ETA is three minutes.

"Come on, guys, our suspect wrecked in a wooded area, and the Lake City Police are asking for back-up. We need to be there when they find him." Max explains.

Everyone in the truck settles their nerves because the chase has not ended for them. They find the last known location of this guy and meet the officer in charge. "We are FBI, ATF, and Atlanta PD. This chase began with us. We are chasing a gun store arsonist, and in our investigation, we met this guy parked on the roadside next to a residence that is a potential target. We lost him after he struck a police cruiser. What can you tell us?" Spencer speaks for the group as everyone shows off their badges.

Lieutenant Fuller recognizes the badges and waves them off. "The driver jumped out of the wrecked vehicle and fled on foot. This patch of land is fifty acres. A timber company began taking down trees last week on the far side. If he makes it that far, he will run out of hiding places." Lt. Fuller stops speaking with the team and replies to a request from his shoulder radio.

"K9 dogs are here, and they will track the suspect. We have a helicopter coming over the highway now. They are monitoring traffic from that direction in case he doubled back. Our air support has infrared cameras, too. With these resources, we will have him captured within an hour. Why don't you hang out in your vehicle? I'll advise you when he is in custody."

The team nods in agreement. After the lieutenant is out of earshot, Tyrone asks the group, "Can we get a look inside this guy's truck? If he is bleeding, we can swab the blood for his DNA."

"Absolutely, we can. Follow me." Spencer walks over to the crime scene techs and asks them if there is any blood in the vehicle.

"None that we've found. Only items of interest are shop rags and trash," one of the crime scene techs replies, then continues, "Oh, and before you ask, the owner reported the truck stolen two days ago."

Tyrone nods and questions the tech. "What type of trash did you find?"

With a puzzled expression, the tech answers, "Receipts for gas, soda bottles, and empty bags of Fritos."

Tyrone asks, "May I take an empty bag of Fritos with me for evidence?"

The crime scene tech pauses. "I don't see why not. There is enough to share." The tech reaches into the truck with a gloved hand, plucks a bag from the stack, and passes it to Tyrone, who places it in an evidence bag. Tyrone turns to the group and grins as he lifts the evidence bag in the air.

"This is our guy. We need him captured, now." Spencer's excitement is palpable.

Tyrone and Spencer walk back to the group and share the news that they found no blood traces, but they have shop rags, empty Fritos bags, and gas receipts. Tyrone shows off his find, too. The team fist-bumps each other. With luck, this guy will be in custody soon, and they can get back home.

The clock ticks as the day moves forward. Lieutenant Fuller shares updates as they come in, but no one can find this guy. The dogs lost his scent at a creek, and the helicopter registers no heat signature. While search team continues for a while longer, they lost hope of capturing this guy. The police issued a BOLO for the suspect, but the description is sketchy since he wears all black.

Mac leans back against the truck and releases a sigh when she hears the likelihood of no capture tonight. Tyrone comes back over to her after he checks on Spencer. "What's the outcome?"

"We lost him. But we know he was trying to make his way to Jerome's house. That leads me to believe he does not know the gun store owner is in police protection. Now, I wonder if he will try again to reach Jerome's house." Mac says with a head tilt.

Tyrone and Mac remain silent as they sort the latest information. Spencer walks over to them after his conversation with the lieutenant. "We got lucky on that one. At least two things went our way—no vehicle damage and no personal injuries. Where do we stand?"

"The truck driver escaped in the woods. With him being at large, what are the odds he will come back to Jerome's residence to start a fire? Do we ask the locals for surveillance on the home? Or do you think we scared him away from Lake City?"

Bradley and José weigh in on the conversation. "We think he'll try Jerome's one more time before leaving the area. Based on his past fires, he has one more day in this area before traveling to his next."

Spencer agrees with the guys and calls Agent Williams for help with the locals. If they can enlist help from the police department, they can go back to the hotel and discuss their options. The group will stay and take part in the stakeout at Jerome's tomorrow night or travel home and let the locals handle it.

After the call to Agent Williams, Spencer relays the extra information to the group and suggests they go to the hotel and discuss their options.

The trip to the hotel is quiet. Mac calls her mom, checking on her dad's health. Visibly relieved after hearing that her dad is on the mend, she goes through the evidence they have on the case. She adds notes to her cards. She needs time to spread them out and dissect the information. Mac is a visual person and likes to see the evidence in writing. A ringing phone brings her back to the moment. She glances at the front seat and watches Spencer silence his phone call. Mac cringes at the thought of Spencer and someone else. She feels eyes are on her, and when she looks around, she realizes Tyrone is watching her reaction to Spencer's call.

Tyrone shakes his head as if to say, "Don't worry about it."

Mac, in return, shrugs her shoulders and thinks. *How can I not think about it? It has been happening more often in the last couple of days. I want to know who he is talking to and why. Does he still love me? He acts like it, but I just do not know anymore. Maybe working together and being in a relationship is not the greatest idea.*

The group arrives at the hotel, exhausted and hungry. While entering the hotel, Spencer receives a call from the local police captain. They started a roving patrol and stationed officers around Jerome's house. They included the street where the alleged arsonist parked earlier in case he returns. Spencer acknowledges the police's effort and advises the group is at the hotel.

When the team reaches the elevators, they plan to rest for thirty minutes and then meet for supper in the hotel restaurant. A hot shower followed by dinner at a nice quiet table in the corner is just what the group needs. After a hearty meal, the team members open notebooks for reference, and the discussion centers on the next potential fire location. It would be nice if the group could predict the next fire and be on the scene quickly. With a map of the southeast US spread on the table, the discussion begins.

"We know the fire-starter is moving north, or at least that is my assumption. From Lake City, would you choose Valdosta or Macon? Or somewhere else entirely?" Spencer throws out his question to the group, then he sits back and waits while each person makes their decision.

All the answers come back with a resounding Macon except for Mac, as she picks Valdosta for the fire-starter's next stop. Spencer asks her to explain her reasoning.

With all eyes on her, she explains, "If he doesn't get the chance to torch Jerome's house, I feel he will stop at the next logical gun store to make up for the miss in Lake City. However, if he succeeds at Jerome's house tonight, he will make it to Macon before he strikes again."

"When you explain it like that, I agree. I want to change my answer to Valdosta." Tyrone states as he answers his phone. The team sits back and waits for Tyrone to conclude the call. "The evidence from Jerome's scene is at the lab and moved to the front of the line. We should have our results tomorrow morning, although I know what started the fire."

"I suggest we notify the local gun store owners in Valdosta and Macon to be prepared when the fire-starter makes another appearance in Georgia. It wouldn't hurt for Agent Williams to notify the police in the respective districts, too." Mac adds as she looks at the team.

Chapter 13

All heads nod, agreeing with Mac. Then José brings up a question that has been bugging him, "Mac, you referenced a while back you think the fires started in Atlanta after the drive-by shooting. Can I ask why?"

Looking through her bag on the floor next to her chair, Mac locates the file folder holding the articles. She hands the folder to José. "Read both articles. My dad saved them when he saw it in the newspaper after they surveilled Hunter. He didn't know how it would relate, but he keeps information on past clients just in case things happen."

José spends a few minutes on the articles. "Now I get it. Until the police released the information to the media on the gun purchase and Hunter's name, the fire-starter would not have been privy to this information." José's head bobs in understanding.

"That's right. I surmise the drive-by shooting in Atlanta is the trigger. We haven't investigated it yet. We keep following the fires. I want to speak with the shooting survivor, too." Mac adds as she glances at her ringing phone.

"Spencer!" Mac yells as she shows the caller ID on her phone.

Mac answers the call and then listens. "Yes, I'll take the call." Then silence as the operator connects Mac with Willie. Mac's insides are jumping as she has prayed for this call. Willie can identify the shooter, and Mac wants to talk to him.

The group quiets down as Mac talks with Willie. With Mac explaining her theory on the shooting, Willie's knowledge has the potential of breaking this case wide open. Fidgeting in their seats, the men wait for the conversation to end. When the call ends, Mac faces them with a smile.

"Willie agrees to divulge the shooter's name, but his safety in jail and on the street concerns him once he gives up the shooter. He wants protection, and I can't blame him. I'm not sure the fire-starter would target him, but the shooter might. Furthermore, the firebug might not care about Willie, only the fires. I'll discuss with Williams and see what we can work out. Williams needs an update from us, anyway."

"Great news, Mac. You stated from the start that Willie knew the shooter. When is he going to tell us?" Spencer inquires.

"As soon as I can confirm protection, he promises he will share. Willie knows we are out of town. He said he would speak with Williams until we return home."

Mac's bouncing knee gives away her nervous energy. With pen in hand, Mac updates her cards. She picks up the articles again and rereads them. As many times as she has read them, she should have them memorized by now. If the article names Hunter, the other store owners are just that—gun store owners. There is no known relation between them, other than Henry and Hunter's strange relationship, which seems to be a fluke.

"Have we received any follow-up on Simon Burden? Or, with the shooting survivor?" Mac asks with her head down.

Bradley answers, "Nothing yet. José and I expect news this afternoon on Simon, but it hasn't arrived yet."

"I'll call Williams about the shooting information when I ask about Willie. I'm heading up to my room unless you need me." Mac explains. Willie can lead to new possibilities for the case, and she wants Williams to know the story before he gets involved with Willie's protection.

The men wave her off, and she exits the restaurant. As she reaches the lobby area, she bumps into a middle-aged, well-built guy wearing a stocking cap covering his hair and ears. He apologizes for bumping into her, and she does the same. While standing at the elevator, she watches the guy out of the corner of her eye as he exits the hotel. Mac ditches the elevator and walks outside through the lobby, looking around the parking lot. Spencer spots her as she passes through the front doors.

"Where is Mac going? I thought she was going to her room so she could call Williams." Spencer questions the men as his gaze follows Mac until she slips out of his eyesight.

"It looks like she is headed to the parking lot. I'll go see what's going on while you finish up here." Tyrone states. He stands and grabs his bag.

By the time he makes it outside, Mac is out of sight. He walks to the end of the lot and looks both ways. Tyrone jogs towards the other end of the

119

lot when she rounds the tree at the farthest corner. "What are you doing? It is pitch dark out here." He asks Mac through clenched teeth.

Mac hears the concern in Tyrone's voice, and then the other men walk up behind him wearing quizzical expressions. "I bumped into a guy wearing a stocking cap as I was leaving the restaurant. He wore his cap pulled down over his ears, and I thought it was strange, so I came out here to see if I could find a truck in the lot. I didn't find a truck nor the man. He walked so fast I never saw him after he exited the hotel. So, we can go back inside."

No one speaks as they make their way back inside the hotel. Spencer advises everyone to go to their rooms for rest. They will reconvene at 0800 for breakfast and then determine their next steps. He also reminds everyone the local police are conducting surveillance on Jerome's house, and if anything happens, they'll call. No one comments as the elevator dings, signaling their floor is next. The foursome part ways as they enter their rooms.

Seeing the guy with the cap downstairs is unsettling for Mac. She can't shake the feeling the guy was their arsonist. She's not sure why, but he is the only other person she has seen wearing a stocking cap that way. Knowing she will soon give in to exhaustion, she calls Agent Williams while she can still muster a conversation.

Agent Williams answers his cell on the first ring. "Hi, Mac, I've been waiting for a call. Let's her your update." Papers rustle in the background as he grabs a notebook.

"Hope you're not in a hurry. We've had several developments since you and Spencer spoke. I have a favor, too. So here goes."

Mac and Agent Williams talk for over an hour. They bounce ideas off one another and then agree on a plan. The favor was not a favor, as Agent Williams states. Protecting Willie is part of the job. Just because Mac feels sorry for the kid doesn't make it a favor. It pleases Mac that Agent Williams will meet with Willie and protect him for as long as necessary. If the situation turns dicey, Williams suggests the WitSec program as an option for Willie. However, that decision will be months down the road. Williams praises Mac for her thoughts regarding the Atlanta shooting as the trigger for the fires. He agrees it makes perfect sense Atlanta is the starting point for everything. Now, Mac asks Williams for help to locate the shooting survivor. She wants to speak with this guy. Also, Williams agrees to notify Valdosta and Macon police about the potential gun store fires.

Finally, after their call, Mac takes a hot shower and climbs into bed. With pen in hand, she makes her follow-up list for the case. The first item is Willie, as Agent Williams will contact him tomorrow. If Willie divulges the shooter's name to Williams, they can investigate that person and see where that leads. Next is Simon Burden. He doesn't exist except as a name on a bank account. Before she finishes for the day, she logs onto the FBI database and requests a background on Jerome Taylor. The background comes back quickly. It is clean, and it confirms he is a Federal Firearms dealer, and he holds the appropriate license. Mac takes a deep breath to settle herself. She reaches over to turn the lights off, and sleep takes over within minutes.

Several hours later, Mac's cell phone blares. Bounding out of bed to stop the awful noise, she answers. "This better be excellent news, Spencer."

"Well, good morning to you, too."

"Is it morning already? I just closed my eyes."

"It's early morning. It is 0230. We have a fire to see. Be downstairs in five." The call ends.

As Mac staggers to the bathroom, her mind races. How could Jerome's house be burning, or is it even Jerome's house? Didn't they leave police officers on surveillance duty? She runs a brush through her hair and whips a rubber band around it, creating a ponytail, while dressing. Then she steps into her boots while grabbing her phone, weapon, and badge from the nightstand. Five minutes later, she walks to the elevator.

"Spencer, you didn't tell me what is burning." Mac grumbles.

He looks around at the group and states, "Jerome's residence."

Bradley and José shake their heads, and Tyrone jumps in to the conversation, "How can that be? I thought the local police had surveillance on it."

Spencer nods in agreement as he speaks, "There is surveillance—or was. A 911 dispatcher received a call about a car accident with entrapment, and the location was so close to

Jerome's, the police surveillance team responded. Of course, while they were away, the fire starts in the garage area. Luckily, the police were not away too long, and upon their return, the fire was visible from the road. They called the fire department, so Jerome is lucky with just minimal damage to the house."

"Who made the call to dispatch? Was it a legit call?" Bradley asks.

"We are looking into that now because it seems the call was a distraction for the fire-starter," Spencer explains.

Everyone enters the vehicle and remains silent on the drive to Jerome's. Without traffic at this time of day, the commute is short. Tyrone wants to get a first look at the fire. He prays for usable evidence. His goal is to find something to tie all fires to the same person. That's his reason for following the fires up and down Interstate 75.

When they arrive at Jerome's subdivision, the scene is active. Fire department personnel, ambulance, police, and neighbors gather in the street in front of the house. The police have spoken to the neighbors, and no one saw anything. With the time of night, that is understandable. The fire department captain walks with Tyrone to the back of the house and shines a flashlight on the burned area. Tyrone knows what to look for as he walks over to the trash can. He peers inside, and he wants to jump for joy. His camera flashes with a high-intensity flash as he captures pictures of the contents and the can itself.

Tyrone's evidence collection continues as he ambles around the exterior of the home. He spends several hours doing what he does so well. "Hey guys, can you come back here?"

The other team members walk toward Tyrone, but with the fire department's bright lights, it is hard to see the path. The flood lights illuminate the surrounding area, making it appear like daytime. As they walk into the light, it's blinding, even holding their hands above their eyes.

"What's up, Tyrone?" Bradley arrives first, wiping his eyes.

"Our firebug left us evidence of a mistake. I have proof of the Fritos. Look in the trash can." Tyrone points to the can in question as he grins.

Each person walks over to the trash can and peers inside. All lift their heads with gigantic smiles. "It's about time! How soon can we dust for prints? This fire destroyed this can, but the second one is still intact. It's scalded in a few areas, but I hope we can pull some good prints off it. The problem is, I need to take the whole can in for evidence."

"No problem, we'll have the local police handle the shipment. They can bill us. I'll make it happen." Spencer jogs over to the lieutenant on duty and explains the situation. Without hesitation, he agrees to whatever is necessary.

Tyrone wraps the waste bin for transport and turns it over to the police lieutenant. He removes a few of the chip bags for his own analysis. Not that he is better than the rest—it just makes him feel better knowing he can testify to his own work.

They return to the hotel for a few hours of sleep and agree to meet over a breakfast of waffles and bacon. Everyone is on time for their breakfast meeting. The late-night rendezvous has their stomachs rumbling for food. During breakfast, they discuss the fires, and the team selects Macon as the next logical location for a fire. If the team can't get in front of this firebug, they may chase him across the country forever.

With bags loaded into the truck, the group sets out for Macon. While en route, Agent Williams calls Mac and advises the shooter was Timmy Tanner based on Willie's statement. Atlanta PD will protect Willie once they release him from jail later today. Also, Timmy Tanner's whereabouts are unknown. Detectives with Atlanta PD could not locate Timmy anywhere in the city. None of his friends claim to have seen him in a while. Timmy's girlfriend wants to make a missing person report, but she hasn't shown at the precinct yet.

Mac explains to the guys about the happenings with Willie after her discussion with Agent Williams. Also, she shares the shooter's name with everyone. Bradley has his laptop open and plugs in the name Timmy Tanner. Then he sighs.

"Not much information on Timmy Tanner from Atlanta. I thought this guy would have a rap sheet longer than two arrests," Bradley states. "Maybe I should use Timothy." Bradley reentered the name as Timothy. "Oh yea, this is what I'm talking about. He has arrests for drugs, theft, burglary, weapons, and this guy is young. This lifestyle began early in his childhood. He dropped out of high school just recently. He and Willie attended the same school."

José pipes up, "It sounds like he is underground. He's probably staying with friends or family. See if you can track down a relative or something. If we make it back to Atlanta, we can knock on some doors instead of riding up and down Interstate 75."

"I sent a request to records to see if they can find a relative for us," Bradley states as he continues to search the internet.

Mac answers her cell and listens to the caller. The guys watch as Mac's face turns into a smile. It's Willie calling. That much they can figure out. They talk for fifteen minutes. Once the call ends, Mac shares Willie's statement with the group. "Willie said that Timmy was a friend from school. He is a white guy trying to make it with black friends. Timmy kept telling Willie he wanted to prove himself to the guys. When Timmy shot at those basketball players, it surprised Willie. Timmy didn't tell Willie beforehand of his intentions, and Willie didn't know Timmy had a gun. After the shooting, Willie heard one guy died, but that is all he knows. He doesn't even know the dead guy's name."

There is silence in the truck as the men digest the information Mac shared. "Sounds plausible to me," Spencer interjects. "At least Willie will be safe until we get this figured out."

The note cards come out of Mac's bag, and she adds the latest information to the stack. Tyrone asks Mac to read the latest updates aloud to the group. They can discuss and think about what they know. She complies with Tyrone's request. Mac reads them, and then José speaks. "We still have no definitive answer on Simon Burden or Timmy's location. My question is, once we find Timmy, how is he going to help us with the fires?"

Spencer explains that if the trigger is the drive-by shooting, Timmy might help put the puzzle pieces together for them. Even if Willie thinks the drive-by was happenstance, Timmy could have been targeting one guy without Willie's knowledge. They need to know if there is a relationship between Timmy and the deceased or any of the survivors.

After a few hours on the road, Spencer takes an exit for gas and food. "I'll pump the gas while you guys take a break inside. Do not loiter. We are getting back on the road so we can be in Macon by nightfall. If there is a fire in Macon, we'll be there. Someone needs to search for hotels on Interstate 75 with easy access to main roads."

"Yes, sir." Bradley waves at Spencer as he enters the convenience store with a grin on his face. "I have done nothing today but ride, and I'm starving," Bradley says to anyone listening.

The group splits at the front door, each going in different directions. Mac goes straight to the ladies' room while the men head for food and drink. As she passes the chip aisle, she notices a female patron with a stack of Fritos and various chips in her hand. Mac hangs back from the lady and waits to speak with her when a group of ten youthful girls comes out of the ladies' room, screaming and talking. Apparently, she is buying snacks for the girls. Mac settles her heart as she takes her turn in the restroom.

When she gets back to the truck, the men already have their seats. "How in the world do you guys get finished with everything in such a hurry?"

"Come on, Mac, you know it doesn't take guys long. It's a natural thing." Tyrone explains to the group and laughs.

"Thanks, Tyrone, for clearing it up for me." Mac buckles her seatbelt when Spencer's phone starts his horrible ringtone. Everyone knows Agent Williams' unique ringtone of sirens.

"Agent Williams, the group, is here, and you are on the speaker," Spencer answers.

"If you are north of Valdosta, turn around. There is a fire burning right now."

"Now? It is still daylight. This makes little sense. Why is he setting fires in the daytime? Was anyone in the gun store when the fire started?" Mac asks.

"No one was inside the shop. Two cars belonging to customers were still in the lot. They claim they saw nothing. The owner, Toby Jesup, closed shop early today because of a dental appointment. His wife is Jill, and they live two miles from the shop on five acres. I haven't heard from the local police yet on her whereabouts," Williams continues.

"Send us the address, sir. Spencer will turn this baby around and head back south." Bradley suggests.

"Mac, the address is coming to your phone." Williams ends the call without a closing word.

With the address entered in the GPS, they head back south. Mac's insides twist in anxiety. She wants and needs to be with her family since her dad is recovering from surgery, but she must continue tracking this sick person by setting fires. Between her dad's operation, the fire-setter, and Spencer's secrets, her nerves are getting the better of her. She stares out the car window, trying to determine the reason for the change in the fire-starter's MO. It makes little sense for him to start a fire in the daytime when the others have been at night. Is he changing things up? Is this a copycat? They can't afford another firebug. Mac notices her team members' somber moods. None of her teammates speak since it disappoints everyone to be traveling to another fire. They just discussed the possibility of going home earlier this morning.

As Mac steps out of the truck in Valdosta, the heat envelops her. "It's hotter here than Florida." She raises her jacket to get air circulating throughout her body.

"It is drier in Florida and muggy here in Georgia. Strange how they are close in proximity, but the weather patterns are so different." Tyrone explains as he wipes his forehead.

The group meets at the back of the truck, where they search for booties and masks. Fire department personnel, police department, and ambulance crews are still on the scene. Tyrone takes the lead this time. He shares his ideas, and the rest of the team follows. The store is a total loss. It was a stand-alone wood-framed building on a flat parcel of land situated to the side of an older strip center. Delivery vehicles gain access from the rear of the shopping center through an access road when delivering goods. Mac jots a note on her pad regarding this access road because she wants to compare this to other centers. Her idea of a truck driver still resonates with her.

The team produces their credentials to gain entrance to the burned building. The walls have fallen inward, but the origins of the fire are noticeable in the debris. Tyrone points out that this fire was hotter than the others. The firebug is using more gas now, which means he is escalating. He gestures around the burned area. "Where are the owners? They need to be in police protection, and we need to meet with them and ask them a few questions."

Detective Simpson walks up to the group and introduces himself. He explains his captain spoke with Agent Williams earlier. Simpson is the lead fire investigator for the city police department. He has the owners at their house right now, waiting until he meets with the group. The team agrees to follow the detective to the Jesups' home, which is two miles from the store. The detective advises it will be hard to protect the owner at his current residence since it sits on five acres off a one-lane road.

Spencer urges the detective to contact his captain and make other arrangements to protect the owners. "In the past, the arsonist targeted the owners within 48–72 hours after he torched the store. We would like a surveillance team to help us with the residence. The owners need not be there."

"Toby Jesup is angry, or a better word is ballistic. He wants to stay home and hope the guy shows up at his house. If this firebug attempts anything at Toby's residence, I feel sure he will put a bullet through this guy's head and never flinch. He is just that kind of guy," Detective Simpson explains.

Spencer counters, "That's the sole reason Toby needs to stay elsewhere, not that we can force the man to leave his home. But maybe someone can persuade him to leave so we can try surveillance again. Our first attempt did not work out so well. Maybe with additional help, we will get him tonight." Spencer's phone rings. He steps away as he glances at the caller ID and ends the ringing without answering it. When he turns around, he is face to face with Mac.

Chapter 14

After a brief stop at the Jesups', the team travels to the police department. They sit in a conference room, planning their next steps in the investigation.

Tensions rise high as Spencer receives more unexplained calls. The firebug changed his timeline, and everyone wants to go home. The group is irritable as they try to decide on a plan of action. Decisions don't come as fast as yesterday. Agent Williams calls Mac for an update, and she quickly explains the situation. He questions her well-being because he knows she wants to be home with her dad. "Mac, would it best for you to come home? You sound out of sorts, or is there something else bothering you?"

"No, I'm fine. I want to see this through," Mac answers through clenched teeth, wondering if she can hold on that long.

"You know when your heart isn't in a case, unpleasant things can happen, and people can get hurt. I don't want to see that with any of my team. Make sure you get your head straight if you plan on staying a part of this team."

Mac assures Agent Williams she can handle this case without emotions getting in the way. Now, if she could believe that herself, she would feel better. As she looks around the table, every one of her team members wears a scowl on their face. No one is excited about chasing a fire-setter anymore. When the case first started, the team was full of energy and ideas. Now, they have neither.

Detective Simpson enters the room with another man in tow. Simpson introduces him as Lieutenant Ranson of the Valdosta SWAT team. "Lieutenant Ranson has agreed to let us use his team tonight for surveillance on Toby's house. We have already mapped out the positions and vantage points. We will handle the surveillance while you all rest."

Spencer stands, "Rest? None of us mentioned that. We want to be a part of this surveillance team." Everyone around the table agrees with Spencer. "We've followed this guy up and down Interstate 75, and we would like to see the takedown."

"That's not my call. Agent Williams worked it out with our superior. Call him for any changes, since this was not our idea. We are leaving in thirty minutes and will notify you when we have this guy in custody." Lieutenant Ranson turns and exits.

Their heads nod in unison as they acknowledge their boss decided on the nighttime outing. It was actually a relief for the team to have that decision made for them. A solid night of sleep is coming their way, and it's something they've had little of since this nonsense started.

Spencer speaks to the group. "You heard the man. We get the night to recoup some of our lost rest and sleep. Make sure you get some. We don't know how long this case will have us running around the country. Use the rest of the day to follow up on outstanding requests. Load up, and we will go to the hotel."

After his announcement, the members pack their gear and walk to the vehicle. Mac doesn't make eye contact with Spencer. She grabs her bag and heads outside. Her notecards need updating, and she wants to follow up on Willie and the search for Timmy. Agent Williams mentioned neither of them in any of his calls today.

The drive to the hotel is quiet. Once the vehicle is in park, everyone hops out in silence. Spencer yells at their backs to meet for breakfast. Mac ignores him as she takes the stairs to her third-floor room because she is not in a mood to talk with anyone.

A long hot shower awaits Mac, as she needs it to calm her nerves. Just as she wraps her hair in a towel, she hears a knock on her door. Her heart sinks as she is not in the mood for a visit, let alone Spencer. She reaches for the door and stops. "Who is there?" Mac asks after looking through the peephole and finding no one. No reply comes. She glances down at her feet and sees a piece of white paper. Once unfolded, she reads it and smiles. She knows the sender, and it makes her heart happy. Spencer has left a note that simply says, "I love you. Sleep tight."

Mac props herself up on the bed and leans back on the headboard. Why would he leave a note? The secretive phone calls still bother her. She doesn't like the unexplained. Mac sends Spencer a text, repeating his note to herself, and he replies with a red heart. She shoves her issues with Spencer to the side, as she needs to concentrate on this case.

Agent Williams answers Mac's call on the first ring. They discuss the case, and the fact Timmy remains missing. The police still have his apartment, his parent's, and his girlfriend's apartment under surveillance. Mac advises Williams she wants to meet with the survivors of the drive-by shooting. The more she looks at the evidence, it leads back to the shooting. The fires started in Atlanta after the media released Hunter's name and printed it in the paper. Agent Williams is more agreeable now after Mac explains her thought process.

With the call over, Mac lays her head back on the pillow and has no recollection of her whereabouts when her phone blares at four in the morning. She answers groggily, "Yes?"

"Get dressed. The truck leaves in ten minutes. Fire burning as we speak in Macon."

Mac doesn't bless the call with a goodbye as she hangs up on the caller. Thank goodness she keeps her bags packed and clothes ready to wear. Within three minutes, she stands in the elevator, waiting for the doors to open. While she waits for the elevator, the thought crosses her mind. Why not Valdosta when the Jesups' home still stands?

When the doors open, her group is waiting for her to enter the elevator. Mac mutters, "Good morning" to down-turned faces.

The resulting sounds show no one is awake yet except Spencer. He wakes up quicker than anyone Mac has ever seen. "Good morning, Mac. I hope you slept well." Spencer acknowledges her with a light tap on the forearm.

Mac replies with a grunt as she turns to face the doors.

The ride down is quiet. Tyrone waits until the group settles in the vehicle. "What do we know, Spencer? If this is our guy, he changed up his timetable again. He's messing with us."

"Gwen Davies, a widow, owns the gun store. Her husband was killed in service, and she quit her job in finance to run the store after his death. She has a great reputation in the gun industry. Hunter Bows and Gwen have a relationship. She dated Hunter before he married Caroline. The gun store has a fire suppression apparatus that stopped the blaze. The fire-starter should be mad at his choice since the store still stands." Everyone in the truck perks up as Spencer shares the latest intel.

"Are you sure about Gwen dating Hunter? That could prove useful information, Spencer," Bradley adds as he shares a glance with the team.

"I thought you might wake up when you heard the news. No one knows if Hunter's relationship is known outside of the gun world, but it is an interesting tidbit." Spencer travels north toward Macon when the address pops up on his phone. "Another interesting fact is this store is off 475, the Macon bypass. This guy is changing things up now. I wonder why."

Mac elaborates on the theory, "Some perpetrators tire of the chase. They change things around, so they get caught without turning themselves into the police. We can only be so lucky that he wants us to capture him. With the fire this close to home, maybe we will get to visit home for a night."

Tyrone answers for the group, "Mac, you need to make time to see your dad while we are this close. You can always pick us up if the firebug continues north."

"We'll see what happens today. I spoke with Mom and Dad last night. They both said Dad is doing good, getting stronger every day." Mac smiles as she remembers her conversation.

Tyrone reaches across the seat and gives Mac a fist bump. "That's my guy. Your dad was a smart soldier. He could always see beyond the plan. Almost like he knew the future and what the opposition would do to us." Tyrone sits back in his seat as the memories flood his mind.

The group turns silent as Tyrone speaks of his time in the service with Myles. José jumps into the conversation. "I can't believe either of you are still alive. With all you went through and the things you saw, how do you stay sane? I am not sure how I would have handled being in the service. I've seen enough in my law enforcement days and now with ATF, but the service is a whole other level of bad."

"My faith, family, friends, and my job keep me grounded. When things get bad, and I need help to cope, all I have to do is mention it to my wife if she hasn't noticed it first. She knows what to say and when to say it, and if I need medicine, she doesn't hide it. I've learned to accept the fact God gave me her for a reason. When we first got married, I tried to buck her. I even told her I was leaving her because I could not control my dreams or temper, and I didn't want to hurt her. Well, that was two kids and twenty years ago."

Mac's mouth opens as she stares at Tyrone after his personal revelation of struggling with the dreams. "You know, Tyrone, dad has issues with dreams. I can remember waking up in the night to Dad yelling orders to his troops. It is the absolute creepiest feeling. I would run into my parent's room, and Mom would hold and rock him in the bed—anything to soothe the dreams and fears. When Dad gets stressed, he rubs a scar on his forearm, where he took a knife. It almost cut his arm off. The knife wound went to the bone. One of Dad's guys neutralized the evil guy, but Dad still suffers. This is a crazy world we live in now."

With all the personal stories out in the open, the team falls silent again. Each person has a story because everyone has a past, and the past makes them who they are. Mac can't believe Tyrone shared his stories. He seems so in control, but she would not want to make him mad, knowing how he handles himself if the need arises.

Spencer's phone rings sitting on the console, and he answers it from the steering wheel. "We are on speaker, Agent Williams."

"Good morning, Team. The sun should be up soon. Hopefully, that will brighten your day. The owner of the store, Gwen Davies, is waiting for your arrival at the store. Her manager pulled the surveillance tapes. This might be the best lead we have. Go get him and call me after you see the store and meet Gwen."

The call ends as they enter Bibb County, Georgia. They collect their thoughts as they prepare to walk through yet another crime scene. At least there are no deaths or injuries at this scene. Spencer turns into the parking lot amidst the flashing lights of police, ambulance, and several fire trucks.

After they unload, a police officer walks over and instructs them to follow him. As they make their way across the lot, Mac notices the building is nicer than most gun stores, and the front appears renovated. It has an artisan-style look to it with the siding, shutters, and substantial posts. The lot boasts ample parking with easy access to the major road.

The officer introduces the team to Gwen and Detective Reynolds. Tyrone says his hellos and then excuses himself so he and the guys can look at the damage. He suggests Mac speak with Gwen.

"Gwen, do you feel up to answering a few questions?" Mac asks the owner.

"Yes, the sooner, the better. I need to notify my insurance company so we can get started on the rebuild," Gwen states matter-of-factly.

Mac and Gwen speak over the next hour. Gwen shares her history with Hunter Bows. She admits to Mac they used to date, and she would see him at a few gun shows they attended. They still spoke several times over the years, just checking on the other one. Hunter's death was a shock to her. Gwen knows nothing about the stolen gun. Also, Gwen advises Mac she lives in a condo, but it is not under her married name. She doesn't think the fire-setter will come after her since he can't find where she lives. Mac points out that he could be anywhere, including following her. Gwen gives in and agrees to stay with a friend for a few days.

A loud noise makes Mac and Gwen look toward the store. Two firefighters drag a metal ladder to the side of the building. Moments later, Tyrone climbs up the ladder to the roof. There is a brief pause in the activity when he holds up a piece of a plastic can in his hand. "This is our lucky day! We have a partial Molotov cocktail. It looks like this might be the gas can handle. With luck, it will have prints on it."

The group meets at the bottom of the ladder. "Did you find any other evidence in your walk-through?" Mac asks the guys.

José points to several plastic bags with items of interest in them. "Here is the evidence collected so far. Tyrone will have to find an enormous bag for the can. Has anyone looked at the surveillance tapes yet?"

Spencer speaks up. "Not yet. We all need to be present for that show. Are we ready?"

Gwen waves them over to her Chevy Tahoe, and they watch as she cues up the videos on her laptop. The video is so clear it's like they are watching a television show. They watch the sunset behind the building. Cars leave the lot, and a truck enters. Mac's heart pumps hard and fast as she suspects a truck driver as the perpetrator. They watch the large truck park across the lot with no truck cab activity for a while. The group grows impatient, watching nightfall and seeing nothing from the truck. José asks, "Can anyone see the license plate on the truck? It's blurry to me."

Everyone agrees the tag is too blurry to read, then finally, there is action. The driver's door opens, and the driver steps to the back of the truck. Once the back doors are open, he removes several plastic gas cans holding rags in the spout. "Mac, you are right, once again. We have a truck driver setting these fires. Now to find out who this person is and why he is doing it." Spencer states while reaching for his phone. Agent Williams needs to see this.

Mac shrugs off the accolades and describes the truck and the driver. Unfortunately, the driver dresses in all black, from head to toe, and never looks at the camera. The group watches as he makes several trips to the back of the store with the cans. Minutes later, the flame flashes from the rooftop of the gun store, and the driver calmly walks back to his truck, climbs inside, and drives off. This guy doesn't appear nervous or worried at all. He takes his time setting the fire. Then his escape is not hurried either. It looks like the driver slows the truck and turns to check out his handiwork before proceeding.

Once Gwen emails Agent Williams a copy of the video too, the group bids farewell to her, reminding her to stay vigilant and to call them if she notices anything out of the ordinary. The team is excited to go home with new intel. The conversation begins as soon as the truck doors shut.

Tyrone begins, "I have more evidence from this fire since the fire didn't burn long and hot. We have enough to tie this guy to multiple fires. When we find him, he'll go away for a long time." Tyrone rubs his hands together, and he beams with happiness.

After an hour of hashing out the fine points of the latest fire, the group settles in for the drive. The passengers write in their notebooks, sorting out facts. It feels good to go home. Agent Williams calls the team before they reach Atlanta, and everyone holds their breath for fear of another fire. "Team, all is quiet, so go home and rest. We will meet at the bureau tomorrow morning at 8."

Mac spends the last minutes of the ride contemplating Spencer's phone calls. She can't decide if she should confront him or not. It is his choice to date and even date multiple people. She reminds herself they never discussed being exclusive. However, Mac is not into sharing her man. Spencer should have addressed that part of their relationship with her before he did it.

In the FBI office's parking lot, the group waves goodbye as each walks to their vehicles without a glance at the office. Everyone wants to see their families and rest. The downtime will do their brains good and give them a fresh perspective tomorrow.

Chapter 15

As she drives to the office the next day, Mac notices the sky is gray with rain clouds passing by at a top rate of speed. Storms are coming in from the west and will be in Atlanta by noon. Mac is taking the notion of no news is good news as it relates to the fires. Her family dinner is tonight, and Mac is eager to see her dad.

Walking into the office, she notices the silence—the usual buzz of activity is absent. Most of the offices sit empty and dark as Mac passes them on her way to the conference room. She arrives first, which she finds odd. Agent Williams is always at the office early. She often wonders if he lives somewhere on this floor.

Bradley enters soon afterward. "Where is everybody? I thought I was running late."

"Did we miss a memo, Bradley?" Mac asks jokingly, trying to cover her nerves.

"No, you didn't miss a memo. Your team is the only one on the schedule for the day. The rest of the agents are on various assignments," explains Agent Williams, walking in behind Bradley. "Where are the other three? They're late." Agent Williams appears distracted or troubled. Mac and Bradley exchange glances.

"I'm not sure," Mac answers, then continues, "Do you have any information on Timmy Tanner?"

"Not yet. I'll ask you and Spencer to follow up on him if Spencer ever shows up," Williams states.

Seconds later, the three remaining members of the team show up for the meeting. The team shares their evidence with Agent Williams and adds the information to the crime scene book, too. Tyrone works his magic with the evidence collected from the fires, Bradley and José will check in with their boss at ATF, while Spencer and Mac work on the drive-by. After the meeting ends, Agent Williams asks Spencer and Mac to hang back. He would like to meet with them separately.

Spencer sits back down in his chair. Mac takes the chair next to him. With both sets of eyes on him, Agent Williams boldly asks, "What's wrong with you two? You act like something is eating at you. Neither one looks at the other one. If you can't work together, please tell me. I'll have you reassigned in a split second. This case is too important. My suggestion is to get your heads back in the game and solve this thing. Sooner rather than later. You're excused."

Agent Williams walks out of the room without another word, leaving Spencer and Mac speechless. Decision made, Mac asks, "Spencer, I don't like secrets between us, and I feel you have one. Care to explain the secret phone calls?" Mac stares at Spencer while he considers his reply.

"No, I don't, but you shouldn't worry about us. Is that why you've been acting strange over the past few days? Because if it is, there is nothing to worry about. I still want to be together. Can you trust me on this?" Spencer pleads as he reaches for Mac's hand.

"I will until you prove me wrong. But just know, I dislike the unexplained phone calls. It makes me think you're hiding something or someone from me."

"Mac, please believe me when I say it is not another woman. I have the one I want. I love you, Mackenzie Morris."

Her heart flutters as the words exit Spencer's mouth. She loves Spencer, but she doesn't want a life with someone who hides things from her. Mac has a suspicious mind. That's why she excels at her job. "Spencer, I love you, too. I just wish you would have told me about the calls. It makes me uneasy."

"No more worries about phone calls. We need to visit Willie and see if he can give us something we might use." Spencer stands from his chair as his cell phone blares an obnoxious tune. He answers it and grins as he talks to Tyrone. "I'm putting the phone on speaker. I'm here with Mac."

"Hey, you two. I hope you have worked through your issue, not that it's any of my business. Now on to work, results came in on the fiber from three of the fires, and they match. It comes back to a dark green army jacket. I mean a real bonafide army jacket. Our dude was in the Army for real, or he purchased the jacket from a second-hand store."

Mac ponders this bit of information. "That is interesting, Tyrone. We didn't notice any patches on the video from Gwen's fire, did we? I don't remember any."

Neither of the men recalls a patch on the guy's jacket. The call ends a minute later. "So, did the entire team think something was wrong between us? I suppose I didn't pay enough attention." Spencer comments sheepishly, realizing he needs to get his head cleared.

"Tyrone asked me about our relationship. He said it seemed strained to him, and I agreed. I questioned you, our relationship, and how I could continue being with you if I couldn't trust you."

"I didn't realize it was that serious. There is no way I would cheat on you. Besides, your dad would make sure I didn't!" Spencer spreads his hands with his palms up and out in front of him.

A hearty laugh is what Mac needs. Her spirit lifts after their talk. "I'm having dinner with my family tonight. Want to come with me?"

"If your mom doesn't mind, I'd love to," Spencer leans over and places the softest kiss on Mac's lips. Then he rubs her shoulder.

"Before we go to your parents, let's take another look at Gwen's video. I would love to find patches on the guy's jacket. That could help us identify him."

The keys click on Mac's laptop. "I have the video here. Two seconds and we can view it." Within seconds, the video begins.

Both lean into each other while trying to pay attention to the video. They watch it, but their minds are on each other. Spencer takes Mac's chin and turns it toward him, and kisses Mac again. "Time to leave for your parents. Since no patches are visible, we can discuss us and the case during the travel time."

Dinner at Mac's parents is fantastic, and the food is delicious as always. Her dad's recovery is remarkable. It even surprises Spencer to see Myles outside playing with the dogs when they arrive. Myles doesn't look at all like someone who recently had heart surgery. He throws the ball like a high school football player.

Myles questions the duo about the case. Mac starts with the updates showcasing Willie and Timmy Tanner. Then Spencer continues with the latest evidence collected from Gwen's fire. Myles wonders about this one since the ATF involved his company with surveillance.

On the drive home, Mac and Spencer decide to visit Willie the next day since Timmy Tanner is still MIA. They hope Willie can give them another avenue to follow in locating Timmy. Agent Williams is working with Atlanta PD to find the survivors of the drive-by shooting. It would be nice if he could produce that information while they're in town. Mac explains her idea of the drive-by shooting being the trigger to this mess. Once she hit the highlights, Spencer agrees with her logic. The chronological order of events follows the fires. If Timmy Tanner doesn't show, the survivors will give us some idea of where to look for the perpetrator.

The next morning, Mac wakes up with a smile on her face and the sun shining through her bedroom window. Spending time with her dad and Spencer was just what Mac needed. She is ready to start her day, and it is nice being home. Today, she and Spencer will meet Agent Williams before visiting Willie. They must get approval to see Willie since he is still in protective custody. Agent Williams arranges the meeting for after lunch.

Spencer stops in front of Mac's apartment thirty minutes later, sporting a grin, and Mac asks, "What's the grin for this morning?"

Spencer glances over his left shoulder as he pulls out of the lot into traffic. "Looking at you will make any man smile. You look great. Thanks for our time together last night. It's always nice seeing your family. I needed time with you too."

"Shucks, Spencer. Thanks. I enjoyed last night too. I'm glad you went with me." Mac reaches over and places her hand on his arm laid over the console. They ride in silence for several minutes until Spencer's cell phone blares.

"Good morning, Agent Williams."

"Are you okay, Spencer? You sound funny," Agent Williams asks with a snicker.

"Yes, I'm fine. Mac is with me, and you are on speakerphone."

"Good. Now I only have to say it once—still no information on Timmy Tanner. I approved your visit with Willie. Also, I have the names of the survivors from the drive-by shooting. If you are coming by here, I'll pass along the folder with the background information."

Mac pipes up, "We're fifteen minutes away from you. We'll stop by your office. Thanks, Agent Williams. I appreciate your efforts in finding this information for me. Spencer might need convincing the shooting perpetuated the fires, too. He still questions the motives."

"We'll talk when you get here." Agent Williams ends the call in record time.

Bradley and José meet the duo outside of Agent Williams's office, eager for an update. They exchange pleasantries as they enter the office. Agent Williams sits behind his massive mahogany desk with a phone to his ear. With a piece of furniture that size, you would think the person on the other side would appear small, but Agent Williams is not tiny. He is a rock-solid guy. He joined the FBI after his stint in the service and continues his regimented work-out routine.

They settle in while Agent Williams finishes up his call. He places the handset in the cradle and grins. "We have a fresh lead on Timmy Tanner. An Atlanta PD detective remembers working a case involving Timmy, and he has a friend or cousin who lives in South Georgia. They are following the lead. Enough about Timmy until we hear otherwise. Share your updates." Just as Agent Williams starts the meeting, Tyrone enters the room and squeezes into the last remaining chair.

With the entire team together, two hours fly by. Mac reminds Agent Williams of her meeting with Willie this afternoon. She explains Willie probably has nothing else to add to the investigation, but she doesn't want him feeling left out either.

Agent Williams speaks up, "Before you hit the road, I have some information you might like to hear. The survivors of the drive-by shooting are Bobby Broth and Dean West."

"Unbelievable. You got the names. I want to interview them as soon as possible, Agent Williams. They may have information on Timmy Tanner, too," Mac explains. She writes the names down on her pad.

"Let me give you the rest of the file. Bobby and Dean are friends, along with a kid named Jeremy. Jeremy died in the shooting while Bobby took a bullet in the leg. They all went to high school together. Based on the report, the three guys did not know the shooter, nor did they recognize the vehicle. The guys were playing basketball on an outdoor court when the shooting occurred."

Spencer finishes up his notes, then asks, "Does the report mention spectators?"

Agent Williams glances at the papers in his hands, looks up, and replies, "None reported."

"Can we schedule interviews for today? Maybe they can come to the office for us. We can hold off on visiting Willie. I'll call him and let him know we are still working on the case," Mac advises. She feels Bobby and Dean can offer more information than Willie, and they must pursue that avenue first.

Mac calls Bobby and Dean and explains they're investigating the incident. With some persuasion, Bobby and Dean arrive at the FBI office at 1:00 pm. They appear a little nervous, but that jaw-dropping FBI seal on the lobby floor often has that effect. Once they pass the security checkpoint, a guard escorts the men to the conference room, where the team sits around the conference table.

Mac greets the guests as they enter and steers them to the head of the table. The guys thank the team for working on Jeremy's case. No one from the police department has been to speak with them for a while. Mac explains the reason they are visiting today. The group suspects the drive-by shooting is the trigger, and the recent gun store fires are connected. Bobby and Dean look at each other like they share a secret.

"Do either of you know the fire-starter? Because, if you do and you do not share, we can arrest you as accomplices," Mac states.

"No, ma'am. We know nothing about that. We've bounced around ideas why we haven't heard from anyone lately on the case. That's all," Dean explains as sweat beads on his upper lip.

The interview begins with Bobby sharing some background information with the team. He explains the relationship between himself, Dean, and Jeremy and how they have been friends since high school. They were always together outside of school and work. Jeremy worked to pay his way through school, while the other two were more fortunate. Bobby described his own injury. The bullet entered his lower leg, and he spent weeks in rehab. The doctors were not sure he would ever walk again, let alone play ball. Since he walked into the room, it is obvious the doctors were wrong. However, Bobby is still in physical therapy for his leg. Dean sustained no injury in the shooting.

Spencer asks the guys if they remember seeing anyone else at the court. Dean points out there were several people at both courts, but when the gunshot rang out, everyone ran. Bobby adds the tidbit that his dad was there that day.

José jumps on the fact that Bobby's dad was at the scene. "What did your dad do after the shooting, Bobby?"

"Dad tied a tourniquet around my wound to slow the blood loss. Then he tried to help Jeremy by tying a tourniquet using a belt around his chest. Dad stayed with me until Mom arrived, and then he left. I live with Mom, and they have a unique relationship," Bobby says with his eyes down turned.

"Another hard question to ask. Did Jeremy die at the scene of the shooting?" José questions.

Dean answered for them, "No, sir, Jeremy did not die at the scene. The doctors described Jeremy's injury as unrepairable, and he died on the operating table. When the bullet hit the collar bone, it exploded and bounced around Jeremy's insides, destroying several vital organs."

Both kids try not to show emotion, but when Dean explains the details of Jeremy's demise, they can't contain the tears. Mac places a tissue box in front of them. The team gives them space to regroup. Once the boys calm, Bradley questions them about the shooter. Neither one can ID the shooter, nor can they describe the car.

Bobby asks the team if they have arrested anyone for Jeremy's murder. Bradley advises the investigation is still ongoing, hoping that ends the questions about Willie. He doesn't want to share information that could hamper the trial. But then he changes his mind about Willie.

"Do either of you know Willie Simmons?" Bradley asks.

"Yes, we both do. He went to high school with us. As far as I know, he causes no trouble. Willie was always one of those polite kids. He still says, 'sir and' 'ma'am.'"

Mac ends the interview with the last question for the guys. "If Bobby's dad witnessed the shooting, is he the person who identified the car involved?" Mac holds her breath while waiting for the answer.

Bobby and Dean replied, "Yes," to Mac's question in unison.

Chapter 16

After the interview, an officer escorts the guys out of the FBI office building while the team remains in the conference room. Mac adds additional information to the board and her cards. "I still think the fires have something to do with this shooting. What do you think?"

José breaks the silence. "I'm leaning with you, Mac. It is the only explanation. We still have no identification on our Simon Burden. He doesn't appear in any of the background services. Nor has the bank produced the video showing his face when he opened the account."

Next, Tyrone adds his perspective. "Once we capture this guy, we'll have enough indisputable DNA evidence to place him at the scene of the fires. I just need a match. The DNA isn't coming back with a match in our system, which I find odd if he is ex-Army."

"José and Bradley, continue your search for Simon. Tyrone, Mac and I will visit Jeremy's parents. Tyrone, you can ride along with us or work on whatever is needed." Suggests Spencer.

José and Bradley leave the room and head to their temporary desks in the FBI building. Hunter Bows' financials sit in a tall stack, taunting the team as they'll have to spend the rest of the afternoon going through them."

Finances and love are the drivers of most criminals. Hunter Bows is intelligent with his business ventures or he is hiding something. The guys are determined to locate Simon Burden and uncover for Mr. Bows' financial blunder.

Tyrone excuses himself as well, stating he has reports waiting for his attention, which leaves Spencer and Mac. "Grab your jacket. We'll eat lunch and speak with Jeremy's parents. We have an hour and a half before our visit." Mac is hungry, so she follows Spencer's lead.

The duo eats lunch alone, which is something they haven't done in a while. They enjoy it until Mac brings up the investigation. Spencer still doesn't see eye to eye with her on it. Maybe after the visit with Jeremy's parents, he will see the bigger picture. The duo ride in silence to their next stop as Mac prepares her questions for Jeremy's parents.

Before Mac knocks on the front door, Mrs. Kinds opens it wide. She greets the duo with a tired face. Grieving a child or family member can do a lot of damage to one's appearance and outlook on life. Mac was not expecting Mrs. Kinds to be so late in her years. Mr. Kinds appears behind his wife's left shoulder and invites the agents inside.

Mr. and Mrs. Kinds step away from the door and motion for the duo to take a seat in the sitting room. Mac glances around the room, trying not to be noticeable. Two sofas face each other with a rectangle coffee table in the middle. Built-in bookcases adorn the end wall, and mementos of Jeremy's school days fill the bookcases. Spencer follows Mac's stare, as both see Jeremy from the age of one to death. Life is strange sometimes. A parent's worst nightmare will always be a phone call or a police officer stopping by in the middle of the night saying a child has been in an accident, no matter the outcome.

Mac's emotions are getting the best of her as she tries to ask questions. An hour passes, and they are no closer to answers than when they arrived. Mr. and Mrs. Kinds admit knowing Willie from when the boys were in high school. They agree Willie didn't pull the trigger. Jeremy didn't have any enemies, nor had he received any threats. The only question Jeremy's parents have is why someone would kill Jeremy and neither agent could offer an answer to their question.

"I'm glad to be out of that house. That is such a sad place, Spencer. Jeremy was an outstanding person in all aspects of his life, based on his parent's description. This sounds like a wrong-place, wrong-time shooting. It doesn't appear Jeremy was the target. He was playing basketball when the shooter snuffed out his life." Mac sniffs as she finishes talking.

"Mac, I agree with that part. I'm still trying to accept the connection between the gun store fires and the shooting." Exasperated, Mac stares at Spencer.

"Oh, Spencer. I've explained it to you. Take my cards and go over the evidence by yourself in a quiet room. You'll see the entire picture. I promise. Now, take me back to the office. I want to get my car and go home."

Spencer doesn't respond. Once they climb inside, he turns the vehicle toward the FBI office building and drives away. After a prolonged silence,

Spencer interrupts Mac's thoughts. "You're mad at me again. Your cards are precious to you. You never let them out of your sight, but yet, you are telling me to take them with me. What's wrong now?"

Mac turns her head in astonishment at Spencer's tone. "Why do you assume something is always wrong with **me**? You know, it could be **you** with the issue. Fine, I'll take my cards with me. Let me know your idea on the case and what course we should take or if we should split up the team and go in separate directions."

Now, Mac's rebuttal surprises Spencer. "Wait for just a second. I just asked you a question. It had nothing to do with wanting to go separate ways. Maybe I came across a little crass, but this case frustrates me. We should have solved it by now."

"You realize we've spent a ton of time on the road chasing after this guy. What we need to do is get in front of him instead of following him. That is my sole reason for wanting to work the drive-by shooting case. I know there is a connection," Mac states, realizing she is not one to back down.

Mac watches as Spencer settles down. His facial features soften, and his grip loosens on the steering wheel as he glances at Mac and says, "You're right. The drive-by shooting and the article must be the trigger for the fires. Somehow, we need to find the firebug. Something connects the fire-setter to the shooting somehow. Otherwise, what would be his reason for the fires?"

"Do you think Timmy Tanner is the fire-starter? He is the only person of interest other than Simon Burden who is missing. We know it is not Willie. Hunter Bows is dead, and he sold the gun. The original owner reported it stolen. He would have no reason to start fires."

Spencer's cell phone blares as he turns into the parking lot of the FBI office. He looks at it and knows something is wrong. "Grab your stuff. Agent Williams is calling. If he is upstairs, we will meet him in his office." As soon as Spencer answers the phone, Agent Williams's voice booms through the speaker.

"Where are you? There was another fire last night in Nashville, Tennessee."

Mac advises they're in the parking lot and are heading up to his office. Once the call ends, Mac says, "He seems pretty uptight. It sounds like this case is bothering all of us. Wonder if he notified the rest of the team? If so, we can get a head start on the travel."

Agent Williams talks with Spencer and Mac about the latest fire. Cliff Prater works at the fire department, and he waits for their arrival. The other team members should join them at any moment. The meeting appears over since Agent Williams stops speaking, and he picks up papers from his desk.

"Any word on the store owner? Were they in the store when the fire started?" Mac asks, curious because he mentioned nothing related to the owner.

"No idea. I found out about this fire through the grapevine. Not sure why no one notified us last night, but I intend to find out. Let me know when you arrive. Cliff requests you call his cell phone anytime, day or night, and he will meet you at the scene." Agent Williams's phone rings, and he answers immediately. "I need to take this," he says as he places his hand over the receiver. "Can you close the door on your way out?"

With that statement, Spencer leads Mac into the hallway. "Agent Williams is acting strange. Something is going on, but he isn't sharing."

"I don't know about you, but I can't handle having anything else to worry about. My brain is full. If you need to know, you can ask him later. We need to get the guys and head north."

The rest of the group steps off the elevator just as Mac and Spencer round the corner. "Hold that elevator. We're going down," Mac instructs. Tyrone grunts as the door catches him at the elbow. Then he steps back so Mac and Spencer can enter.

"Thanks, Tyrone. We'll fill you in on the ride, which will not take long, that is for sure. Agent Williams provided little intel."

The team loads up into Spencer's vehicle again for another road trip. This group kept packed bags for events like this. This time, they travel north, and they discuss little about the case. Everyone naps while they can. The trip is uneventful. Without knowing what they were about to walk into, there is not much to discuss.

Mac works on her note cards, Tyrone handles emails and reports on other cases while Bradley and José sleep. Spencer drives since driving is a passion, and he enjoys being in control. Mac relaxes until they arrive in Nashville.

Cliff stands in the store's lot looking irate as Spencer parks the Suburban. Mac states, "I hope he never gets mad at me. With a look like that, he would make a great crime deterrent."

"Let's see what he has to say." Spencer introduces the group to Cliff, and he shakes hands with everyone. "Tell us what you know, and we would like to look inside if we can still see. Otherwise, we will wait until morning."

Pointing to the store, Cliff says, "If you want in today, better do it now. It is getting dark quickly. I'll show you what I can. Come on." He turns and walks to the store.

The group follows Cliff to the storefront. Booties and masks sit next to the front door of the store. The group steps inside, and the retail space appears untouched except for the odor and water puddles on the floor. "This is amazing, Cliff. The other stores we have visited experienced severe damage or were destroyed. How did you put the blaze out before it reached the retail store?" Tyrone questions.

"My cousin was here at the time. It was freak timing. Let me show you around, and then I'll give you all the low down." Cliff turns his back on the team and heads to the rear of the building.

Tyrone steps inside the damaged area of the building. He glances at all four sides before he looks at the floor and completes the same sweep. Within minutes, he places evidence tags on several areas of the floor right under a massive hole in the ceiling. Thirty minutes later, with darkness falling, Tyrone gathers all the marked evidence.

"Alright, guys, I'm done here. It is too dark to continue, and we need to hear Cliff's story. This fire differs from the others, and I don't want to jump to conclusions until Cliff tells us what he knows," Tyrone explains.

Mac steps forward. "Cliff, how about some supper? The bureau will cover it if you can step away for a little while longer."

Cliff speaks into a walkie talkie explaining his situation. The person on the receiving end of the conversation advises Cliff to drive the fire department truck so that if a call comes into dispatch, he can still respond.

A steakhouse comes into view as the convoy turns into the lot. Cliff makes seating arrangements with the hostess, and they sit around a circular table in the back, away from the prying eyes and ears of the public. Mac and Spencer exchange glances when they realize where they are sitting. Cliff is well known here for the server to provide this location.

Once everyone sits, Cliff begins his story. "A little background to get us started. Zac Buttram, the burn victim, is my cousin and business partner. Zac and I own the gun store 50/50. It was my turn to be at the store when the blaze broke out, but I was filling in at the fire department for one of our firefighters. Zac is a sheriff's deputy for Davidson County. We opened the gun store five years ago to supplement our incomes, and we enjoy firearms. I have two children under three, and Zac's wife is pregnant with their first."

"I don't enjoy interrupting, but I need to know if Zac will be okay, especially with the baby on the way," Mac asks as tears well up in her eyes. Mac doesn't normally cry, but this case is a test of wills.

"Zac will make a full recovery, but it will take time. He required skin grafts on his elbow and surrounding area on his left arm from the shoulder to the wrist and another graft on his lower left leg around the ankle. They moved Zac to the burn unit this morning at Vanderbilt Medical Center. Also, with his wife's condition, she has a room in the hospital as well. The baby is due in six weeks, and contractions started as soon as I told her what happened. The doctors stopped her contractions for now, knowing Zac will heal, and she is close to him."

Cliff's details astonish José. The group was unaware of the family details. "Did Zac say anything about the fire?"

"You better believe he did. Zac never lost consciousness, even when they gave him morphine for the pain. He continued to rattle on about the fire. Zac is so mad. I've never seen him like this, not even when we were kids. Zac stated to me and the police that he was in the back, finishing up a gunstock refinishing job for a customer. There was a loud rumble from the road behind the store. The sound was unusual, so Zac stepped towards the store's back when a loud swoosh sounded overhead. He opened the door to hear truck tires squeal out of the lot. When he turned to walk back to the table, the ceiling fell on the counter right next to him. Zac has spent many hours with me and knows how to handle a fire. We have commercial-grade fire suppressors in the store, and he grabbed one to halt the progression. Zac called my cell phone and screamed at me to respond to the store with the fire truck and call an ambulance. Of course, I thought someone suffered a gunshot wound, and I had prepared my station for that, but when we arrived, I saw smoke from the roof. I expected the worst for Zac."

Each member of the group leans back in their chairs. Their adrenaline from the story slows as they take deep breaths. "Can you draw me a map, including the roads and such? Since darkness came quickly, we didn't drive around the area," Bradley poses this question as his mind works overtime. The muscle in his jaw is visible when he is on to something.

With the server delivering their orders, silence overtakes the team. Each pondering their own thoughts and questions. Did Zac see the truck? Were there witnesses in the parking lot or surrounding stores? Was the fire-starter aware of Zac being inside?

After the group consumes the food, Cliff draws a precise map of the building on a white paper napkin. It is a free-standing frame building on an out lot of a shopping center. It has roughly 3000 square feet under the roof with a portion dedicated to retail space, and the remaining space is for storage and workspace. Three sides of the building have roadway access. They primarily use the back of the building for truck deliveries, and this road circles the center. The front and side are available for customer parking.

Bradley takes the map from Cliff and instantly realizes the store is closer to the interstate than he realized. Vehicles have easy access via three sides of the store. The road that winds around the back of the center and the store exits onto the major highway. The perpetrator could have driven around the center, stopped at the gun store, thrown his homemade Molotov cocktails, and then exited onto the main road for his escape. Bradley continues his discussion with Cliff, and they move on to witnesses.

Cliff overheard Zac mention a witness or two, but his mind was not on his conversation. His concern was Zac's wellbeing and making sure he was stable. He knew he would be the one to tell Zac's wife about the situation.

José poses the next question. "Since the gun store owners are the target, can Zac's wife remain at the hospital for a while?"

"Zac's wife has a room at the hospital since contractions began when I told her about Zac. After the doctors stopped the contractions, they felt she needed to stay at the hospital, too. For me, it was an immense relief, knowing they were together. Should I do anything about Zac's house?" Lines etch Cliff's forehead as his voice cracks.

Spencer explains, "We've asked the local sheriff's office to lend a hand with surveillance on both of your homes. Since you are part owner, the arsonist would know that, too. It wouldn't be a bad idea to alert your family of the situation if they could stay somewhere for a couple of days."

"I hadn't thought of my house, only Zac's. My wife and children are there now. I'll call and ask her to go to her mom's for a couple of days. I'm on duty anyway, and I can stay at the station." Cliff looks stressed. The muscles in his jaw are flexing.

Once the conversation subsides, Mac suggests they call it a day, and the group bids farewell to Cliff for the night. They will meet again in the morning before the team heads home unless, of course, the fire-starter strikes again before they get that chance.

The team finds a hotel and they check-in for the night. For once, they may get eight hours of sleep. Everyone takes to their rooms, but with so many things running through Mac's brain, she can't sleep. Her father's health remains a concern for her. Spencer's secret phone calls seemed to have stopped, at least for the time being. How much longer is this firebug going to continue before they capture him? Does the arsonist know about the injuries and deaths? Does he care?

While reviewing her cards, she reads that Bobby's dad was a witness to the shooting. She makes a note to herself to contact him tomorrow for follow-up questions.

Mac doses off to sleep but then jumps out of bed four hours later. What woke her? Is it a sound? There it is again. What is that? Grabbing her pistol from the holster, she rushes to the window. It is only the cab of a semi-truck backing into a space at the hotel. Wonder if that is what Zac heard? It is a low rumble. Mac turns her head and checks the clock beside the bed. Ugh! It is only 4:30 am. There is no way she will fall back to sleep now. So, she opts for a shower and coffee, in that order.

Breakfast is hot and delicious as Mac sits in the room's corner with her back to the wall when her team strolls in to join her. They appear rested and ready for the day. Tyrone is already on his phone as he remains in the doorway, giving him a measure of privacy while he finishes his call. He has a strange expression on his face when he walks over to the table.

"Have we received notice of another fire? One of my guys in Atlanta was in the elevator and overheard that a fire occurred in Lexington overnight." Tyrone shares with the team.

Mac replies with a shake of her head since her mouth is full of bagel. As soon as she swallows, she says, "Check with Spencer. Agent Williams could have called him, but he would have told us. Does it sound like our guy?"

"I'm not sure if it's our guy. My contact did not say what kind of fire. He thought it was strange that another coworker mentioned it at all."

"We will hear soon enough. We are meeting with Cliff again this morning. Maybe he can give us an update on Zac," Mac adds.

Chapter 17

The gun store appears closed instead of damaged until you get close to the door and suck in a breath. The smell of charred wood is unmistakable. Cliff pulls up to the curb and jumps out of his truck. He is calmer today now that things are more settled.

"Hi, Cliff. How are Zac and his wife?" Mac questions.

"Both are stable. The doctors stopped the latest round of contractions since the baby is not due for a few more weeks. Zac is good. He will have to endure two more skin grafts, but otherwise, he'll make a full recovery. He wants to catch this guy. I think we're all lucky he is in a hospital bed, or he might take matters into his own hands."

Spencer shakes his head. "If that is what it takes to keep him out of harm's way, so be it. We'll catch this guy. Did you move your family, too?"

"Yes, we are all set. Let me get you inside the shop. I'm on duty, so if a call comes in, I'll respond." Cliff pulls his store keys from his pocket and turns the lock. Now that he thinks about it, with the back of the building burned and not secure, he is unsure why he locked the door, anyway. He and a few friends moved the merchandise from the store overnight.

Tyrone stands ready with a mask and booties, just waiting for permission to enter. He already mapped his path in his head. Yesterday, when they visited the store, he saw something that required a further look, but he had to wait until daylight. José and Bradley follow Tyrone through the shop to the back door. With the door open, Tyrone halts the guys' progress. "Stop here for a second. I need to check something before your footprints contaminate it. "José and Bradley look around at the floor and the remaining parts of the ceiling. Bradley points at something hanging from a piece of dangling roof cover. "We need to show that to Tyrone. It looks like the remnants of a shop rag. Ceiling sprinklers appear to have worked like a charm."

"Hey guys," Tyrone calls for the pair. "I thought I saw a faint shoe print on the back concrete, but I couldn't confirm it until daylight. It's marked, so walk around it. I'll snap a photo. We need to see if it matches Cliff's or Zac's shoes. If we are lucky, it belongs to the arsonist."

The team continues inspecting the fire site but finds nothing else of use. The shoe print is the most favorable evidence. "Cliff, I have a shoe print I need to compare to your shoes and Zac's if I can," Tyrone explains as he holds the camera in his hand with the shoe print picture.

Cliff lifts his right foot for Tyrone's inspection. "Not a match, Tyrone. Zac and I wear the same type of boots and have for years. But if you want to double-check me, we can go to Zac's and search his closet."

The group joins the conversation. Everyone agrees to accept Cliff's shoes as proof. So, now, they have shoe prints, presumably from the arsonist. This revelation lifts the team's spirits.

"I reviewed the surveillance footage from the night of the fire. You'll find a portion of it interesting. Do you have time to look at it now? I can show it to you on my laptop." Cliff walks to his truck and lowers the tailgate so the team can view the footage.

As the team situates themselves around the laptop, Cliff starts the video. They watch fifteen minutes before the fire until the smoke covers the screen, making it impossible to see anything. After the video ends, the group lets out a sigh. They have a video of someone clad in all black outside the store's rear before the fire breaks out. Tyrone requests a copy of the video, and Cliff agrees to forward it to his email.

"Thanks for your help, Cliff. You've provided us a lot of evidence and insight. We will send the video to our tech group to have them enhance the guy's image. I'm guessing there were no vehicles in the lot last night. The video didn't show any."

"I found no vehicles in the lot before or after. Zac mentioned cars, but the video didn't show any. I wish I had them." Cliff shrugs his shoulder.

Mac speaks. "You did great, Cliff. As Spencer said, your insight is invaluable. We will keep you updated as we move forward in the investigation. Don't let your guard down until we capture this person."

Tyrone is loading his things in the back of the Suburban when Spencer's cell phone rings. The group recognizes the tone and enters the vehicle, waiting for the next assignment. Tyrone takes the front passenger seat so that Mac can work on her cards. While Spencer finishes the call, she prepares her cards. The first card in the stack is the reminder to call Gilbert Broth, Bobby's dad. He has follow-up questions coming his way.

Spencer climbs into the truck and shares with the team their next stop in Lexington, Kentucky. They decide to drive there now because they can be there in a few hours. On the drive, Mac calls Gilbert. He answers on the second ring. Mac questions him for the better part of an hour, learning no additional information. He confirms he was there at the time of the shooting. The boys played basketball at that court two or three times a week. He tried to stop Jeremy's bleeding, but he couldn't. Gilbert blames himself for Jeremy's death, as he should have been able to stop the bleeding.

Mac shares her conversation and her disappointment in not finding any extra information with the others. Her shoulders slump as her mood shifts downward. Every which way they turn, it is a dead end.

The conversation moves to a happier topic with Zac and his pregnant wife in the same hospital. Everyone is overjoyed knowing one good thing has happened from all the sorrow. The ride to Lexington is quick since the traffic cooperated. Spencer's pick for a hotel is a chain hotel that always serves free breakfast. "Let's check-in, grab supper, and enjoy some rest. How does that sound?"

No one answers Spencer. He only receives a few grunts in acknowledgment. As the group unloads the truck, Spencer gets a text. Glancing at it, he slides his phone into his pants pocket. Mac watches but doesn't comment. She remembers Spencer's request to trust him. At this point in the day, she is too tired to worry.

The team separates after supper and retreats to their rooms. Mac enjoys a late-day shower, and then she spreads her cards out on the table. The cards are in a group of viable scenarios. After shuffling them around a few times, she confirms they are no closer to a suspect than the day this chase started. After many days and many miles on this case, the evidence is not there. She is stumped and feels as if they are chasing a ghost. The fire-setter must make a mistake whether it be that someone sees him starting a fire, or he hurts himself.

Mac's frustration grows by the minute. With her head screaming for relief, she pops two aspirin and lies back on the sofa. Since the cards are of no help, she puts them on the table and turns on the television. Watching television is not something Mac does a lot of, so she flips channels, searching for something to hold her interest. Her blood turns cold as she catches the news brief on the Lexington gun store fire. A reporter stands before the store, showing its remnants and stating the FBI/ATF task force would arrive in the morning. The reporter continues her remarks and says the police have a witness to the fire. After she makes the statement, her commentary ends.

Mac grabs a pen out of her bag and jots the reporter's name and the station name. With her headache gone, Mac now has fresh information to start her morning. She promises herself one more notecard review before bed. So, she places them in different stacks and reads them. When she pulls Jeremy's stack to read, she stops and draws a breath. She rereads the card that offers them an obvious clue, but she nor Spencer caught it at the time. The card states pictures of Jeremy were from age one to death. Mac wants to know why there are no infant pictures of Jeremy at his parent's home.

Mac gives into tiredness as she places her stack of cards in her bag. She lays her head on her pillow and pulls the blanket to her chin. That's the last thing she remembers before sunshine breaks through the curtains in her room. She forgot to pull them together before bed. However, when she awakes, she feels the best she has since this case began. She has a renewed sense of purpose for the day, knowing the two reminders are waiting for her. Quickly, Mac dresses and takes the elevator down to breakfast. She is the first of her group to show, so she takes the largest table in the back corner for them. Her eagerness to share the information with the group is palpable. Her feet tap on the floor, and she fidgets in her seat.

Tyrone appears first and notices Mac's increased energy level. "What happened to you last night, or should I ask?" He asks with a wink.

"I have two points on the case that I think will help us solve this thing. When the others get here, I'll share. It pays to have a little downtime." Mac stuffs her mouth with bagel, knowing Tyrone will move along when he sees her mouthful. He is an eater and hates to watch others eat without him.

He meanders to the buffet line, perusing his breakfast options.

A few minutes later, the rest of the group join the table. Tyrone clears his throat before he states, "Mac has information to share. The table is yours."

Mac places her napkin next to her plate after gently patting her mouth. "Two things came to my attention last night. The first is this fire hit the media. A reporter stood outside of the fire-burned building when she stated the police have a witness. I have her name and station name. The second came from Jeremy's card. When Spencer and I visited his parent's house, we noticed childhood pictures on the shelves, but the pictures began around age one. I want to know the reason."

Bradley beat everyone, as he was the first to speak. "I can't believe I didn't turn on the television last night. News shows are my favorite, but I was so tired, I did not even turn it on. I'll call the news reporter if you like," he offers.

"That would be great. Maybe she can drop by the scene and speak with us, too. I'll call Jeremy's parents. Something is out whack with the photos."

José's eyebrows bunch together, and he works his jaw muscles. "Was Jeremy adopted around that age? You said yourself that Jeremy's parents seem older to have a kid that age."

"Could be, José. That is a great reason. I'd like confirmation so I will try them today. If he was adopted, that might not play a role in the investigation, but it will give us answers. Finish breakfast, and we will meet at the truck in thirty minutes."

Spencer's mouth hangs open as he listens to the conversation around the table. He slept last night, and the case never entered his mind while Mac worked. He needs to concentrate on the task at hand. Once he returns to Atlanta, things will be back to normal. Spencer regains his senses and silently thanks Mac for her work ethic.

After the meal, the team drives to the latest fire in anticipation. The gun store owner, Sandy Zuros, is a retired state police detective and will meet them at the store. Agent Williams advises there is minor damage to the building because of the fire-retardant roof covering. There is a gun range attached at the rear of the store, which helped suppress the damage.

Sandy Zuros stands to the building's side as a construction crew covers the hole in the wall. She greets the group as if she is still on duty. Spencer leads and shakes her hand, then introduces the rest of his team. Sandy allows Tyrone permission to enter the building. However, he struggles to hide his disappointment with the construction crew. The crew mutilated any evidence they might have had from that side of the building.

Tyrone mentions this to Sandy, and she calmly brings her cell phone out of her pocket and asks him for his cell phone number. She snapped a ton of pictures and offers to forward them. He obliges her with his number, but it still perturbs him. With her being a retired law officer, she knows the drill about evidence collection. She also offers no excuse for the construction crew arriving before the task force.

Spencer walks into the store with the guys. Mac hangs back to question the store owner. She starts with video surveillance, and Sandy speaks in a high-pitched tone. "I have video cameras. Let me log in and look at it from last night. While I do that, keep asking questions."

Mac continues, "Have you had any customers visit the shop eating Fritos?" From the look on Sandy's face, she must find it the funniest question ever.

"I can't say that I remember one. Why on earth are you asking about Fritos? In all my years with the state police, that never came up, and I thought I had heard everything."

"The arsonist moves on to the gun store owner's residence after torching the business, and he uses bags of Fritos to start the fires. His timetable is between three and five days before he makes it to the owner's residence. Do you live alone?"

"So, instead of potato chips, he uses Fritos. Well, this guy is clever, if nothing else. I found the video. Let's watch." The two women get close to watch the video on a smartphone. As soon as it is over, Mac requests a copy. She saw a shadow of a person matching the image of Hunter's arsonist.

"I know this is a shot in the dark, but are there any other angles from your cameras? The shadow on your video matches another video in our investigation. However, it would help if we could get a picture of his face."

"No, I'm sorry. There is not. I got lucky with the fire damage. When the arsonist threw the Molotov onto the roof, it rolled over to the side, burning a hole in the roof and the wall. But that is all. Since my husband passed, I keep the construction crew on standby. Back to your questions on my living arrangements—yes, I live alone. However, I am not afraid to stay there alone. I have a ranch house with motion sensors in the yard. I'll be ready even if I must stay awake all night. As a matter of fact, I wish he would stop by. I would help you take this guy into custody."

The guys walk up and join the conversation as Sandy speaks her mind about the arsonist stopping at her house. Spencer suggests she reconsider staying alone, but she disagrees, so he drops the argument. He knows you can't win against a woman when she sets her mind. As he walks away from Sandy, he asks, "By the way, Sandy, are you aware of any witnesses to the fire?"

"No. No one came forward to me. The police were here most of the night, but I do not recall anyone mentioning a witness. I'll call the detective handling my case and ask."

Spencer acknowledges her answer and hands her a business card in case she hears anything from the detective that might be beneficial to the case. "You can refer the detective to us if need be."

After the inspection, Tyrone places his materials into the back of the Suburban. He leans against the truck and thumbs through the photos from Sandy. He sees nothing useful, but he'll enlarge the pictures on his laptop to confirm. His mind always circles around crime scenes that he doesn't get to see firsthand. He wonders what he might have found.

Mac suggests they grab a quick lunch and then find a hotel with a conference room or a business center. Jeremy's parents have been on her mind today. Her eagerness to contact them is unbearable.

The group wanders to the vehicle. Mac reminds them about their interviews this afternoon with Jeremy's parents and the news reporter. Spencer drives to a hotel on the interstate, stating it will be easy access if they get called away in the night. Mac doesn't care where they stay, as all hotels are similar. Living out of a suitcase and chasing a fire-starter up and down the interstate is tiresome.

The hotel accommodates the group by providing a conference room. It is large enough for everyone to spread out, so they settle in for the afternoon. Mac waits until mid-afternoon before mentioning the call to Jeremy's parents to Spencer. "We can both take part if we call on speakerphone. I want to hear the conversation, too." Spencer suggests.

Mac places her phone on speaker and dials Mr. and Mrs. Kinds. An old-fashioned answering machine picks up, and Mac waits for the option to leave a message. As soon as she states her name, Mr. Kinds answers the phone. He advises they were receiving so many media calls after the shooting that they screen them all now.

Apologizing for the call, she continues through her statement about the photos. Mr. Kinds confirms Jeremy's adoption at eleven months old, and he shares Jeremy never knew his birth parents. Growing up, he was small for his age and a little behind in learning. With extra work, he excelled and even made it into college. Mr. Kinds cries as he talks about his only child. Mac concludes the phone call and agrees to keep in touch.

After the call, Mac's mood is subdued. She is quiet and reserved while she contemplates the confirmation of Jeremy's adoption. Spencer jumps in to help Mac's mood. "I hear José and Bradley on the phone. If we are lucky today, they can speak with the news reporter about the witness."

"That would be something, wouldn't it? We could use some good news. What do you make of the adoption? Does that change our case any?" Mac questions.

"My question is if Jeremy was behind in learning and growth, was there an underlying reason such as health? They didn't mention any health issues, but we didn't ask either."

"We need Jeremy's autopsy," Mac yells out with a grin.

Chapter 18

Bradley and José end their call with the news reporter. Bradley explains, "Sarah, the news reporter from the fire scene, advises she heard a man speak with the police about seeing a guy dressed in all black come from the back of the building. The witness was driving as he passed the gun store when the man appeared. The man in black kept his head down and his hands in his pockets as he walked along the roadside. Since the witness was driving, he couldn't keep his eyes on the guy. When the witness stopped at the traffic light, he glanced back at the store and saw flames on the side of the building. He dialed 911 and drove back to the scene. The guy dressed in black never showed again."

A moment passes amongst the group while they digest the information before José speaks. "Are there any hotels close to the gun store or another lot where someone can hide a vehicle? The fact the guy walks away proves he drives something, and he hides it close by. Can we ask other shopping centers or stores within a half-mile radius of our burned stores for a peek at their surveillance footage from the night of the fire? It might be a lot of data, but if we see a pattern of vehicles, we might pinpoint the one we are after."

Claps and high-fives reverberate through the conference room. The latest idea encourages the group. Now, to explore the recent possibilities with Jeremy's autopsy and the videos. With so many fires, the group splits the list, and each agent takes their share of gun stores. Using the internet, the agents find the nearest stores most likely to have surveillance cameras. They dial phones over the next few hours. Some stores agree to help, and others require a warrant for the information.

Mac calls Agent Williams requesting warrants for the video footage. He concurs with the group and explains the warrants will be in Mac's email in an hour. With that in the works, she takes a break. Coffee is her favorite drink, and the hotel offers specialty coffees. She slips away from the guys while they talk on the phone. Tyrone is in a heated conversation, his neck veins popping out of his skin. Mac returns to the room with coffee and snacks for the guys. At least Tyrone is calmer now. "Are you okay, Tyrone?"

"Now, I am. An Atlanta lab tech misplaced the ash vial from Hunter's fire. I stayed on the phone while he searched for every available place, and he found it in another tech's batch. The other tech is sloppy, and I have recommended termination, but nothing has happened yet. If he messes with these, I'll have his head on a block." Tyrone expels a huff of air.

Spencer strolls up to the table and takes a coffee, sniffs, and says, "I'll be glad when these videos get here. The videos could prove invaluable. I wish we'd thought of that idea earlier."

The group enjoys an hour of down time until Mac's email gives the famous alert. She clicks her email and sees that Agent Williams has sent over the warrants. She shoos the guys away while she completes her task with the video surveillance.

While Mac is on the phone, the guys receive videos in their email. The excitement builds as the team grows eager to watch them. They begin with the first fire in Atlanta. Several banks and fast-food restaurants provide videos for Hunter Bows' store. Spencer plays the first videos with instructions to write every vehicle in the video. Their goal is to match reoccurring vehicles to multiple locations. With pen and paper at the ready, they watch the video. Silence encompasses the conference room as the group's attention turns to the videos.

Halfway through the first video, the hotel fire alarms blare their ear-splitting sound. Tyrone races to the door and opens it while scanning the lobby. People scramble as they scream for loved ones on their way outside. "We need to pack! The fire must be on the roof!" Tyrone's voice has a tinge of urgency in it that no one takes lightly.

"Roof? Please tell me it's not the roof," Mac stammers with uneasiness in her voice. Although no one could throw a Molotov cocktail onto the roof of a fifteen-story hotel, the thought is troublesome.

"We'll discuss it later. Let's move! We can't afford to lose the evidence we have in this room. The good news is we haven't checked into the hotel yet, so we don't have to worry about getting luggage," Spencer says with a slight grin, "There is always a bright side. You just have to look for it," he continues, hoping his statement calms some nerves.

With the alarm sounding, the group packs the evidence away in multiple bags and boxes. They exit the hotel by a side door right at their vehicle.

Each person turns around and looks at the roof of the hotel. Neither flame nor smoke is visible. They load the evidence into the truck, and the group walks around the building craning their necks to see the roof. On the far side, smoke billows from the roof into the late afternoon sunshine.

"Looks to me like an air-conditioning unit malfunction. The fire department will have this under control in no time," Tyrone explains. "We can eat an early supper while the fire department contends with the mess. But, if the fire closes the hotel, we'll need to find a new one."

The group replies, "A new one?" in unison. José spots a Mexican restaurant across the street in a shopping plaza and offers, "I vote for the Mexican restaurant across the street. I've eaten enough steak for a while."

Everyone agrees, and Spencer drives them across the street. At the table, the team discusses the hotel fire and then the videos. Mac remembers Jeremy's autopsy and asks Spencer, "Did you have time to request Jeremy's autopsy?"

"I haven't called yet, but as soon as we finish eating, I will," Spencer chastises himself for failing to make the request. His head is not in the right place now. Somehow, he needs to calm his mind and hold it together. Other team members glance at him with a puzzled expression. Spencer feels the heat rise to his face. As the lead agent, he should be the one to steer the group to the finish. But his focus is elsewhere.

To lighten the mood, Bradley asks, "Can we stop and buy popcorn? We have ten hours of video waiting for us."

All eyes turn to Bradley as they burst into laughter. "Yes, Bradley, we will get snacks before we tackle the videos," Spencer replies as he shovels a bite of a burrito into his mouth.

After a brief grocery store stop to satisfy Bradley's urge for snack food, they drive 250 yards to the next hotel, which flashes a no-vacancy sign. They drive to the next one on the block, but again, the no-vacancy sign flashes red. Tyrone acknowledges the issue of lodging in this area. "We might need to drive to the next exit if we want to stay near the interstate. With the hotel fire, it may be out of commission for a few days, and all surrounding hotels are at capacity."

Spencer turns the vehicle towards the interstate and hits the gas. There is no lodging at the next two exits. Forty-five minutes later, they sit in another hotel parking lot. Mac's mood crashes as the hotel fire has caused the group to lose valuable time with the videos. Everyone tries to remain hopeful as they walk into yet another hotel.

An hour later, they camp out in a small conference room, barely large enough to accommodate the people and boxes. Spencer cranks up his laptop, and they finish the first video. "How many vehicles did everyone see on this video? I saw eight, but I couldn't name two of them."

Spencer scrambles to write the numbers from each group member. No one recorded the same number of vehicles. "That is interesting, isn't it? How can we not agree on the number of vehicles? We'll use what information we gather from each video and proceed from there." Spencer shakes his head in frustration.

Mac takes it upon herself to write a detailed list of each vehicle from the video. She will gather the information and add it to her plan for matching purposes. The group watches four hours of videos, and everyone's heads bob as sleepiness overtakes their bodies.

Tyrone succumbs first. "I can't watch anymore. My eyes need to close for the night. Mac, here is my list for the last video. What time is breakfast?"

Spencer shuffles papers and releases the group with instructions that breakfast will be at eight. After the room clears, Spencer sits down and calls Agent Williams, not realizing the late hour.

A gruff voice answers and Spencer apologizes for the call. Agent Williams senses something is awry with the caller. "What's wrong, Spencer? Are you all still working?"

"The team retired for the night a few minutes ago, but I need to ask a request of you. I failed to do it earlier in the day. Can you get us a copy of Jeremy's autopsy report? It's a hunch, but we think it could help untangle ideas on the case."

"Sure, Spencer, no problem. I will request it first thing. Now, get some sleep and we'll talk tomorrow." Agent Williams ends the call without another word.

Spencer recoils at how abruptly Agent Williams ends the call. He drags himself to his room and falls onto the bed, still wearing his clothes. A moan escapes his mouth as he struggles to get comfortable. Once he settles, he falls into a dream-filled sleep. His brain jumps from Mac to fires and back to Mac again. At sunrise, he stirs and notices he never changed his clothes before bed. He is a total mess, and he wants to impress the team today. So, he will be the first at breakfast and will relay his phone call to Agent Williams about Jeremy's autopsy.

Breakfast smells terrific as the group wanders into the lobby. With plates piled with food, the team digs in, making breakfast time pretty quiet. The team is traveling to Atlanta today since nothing transpired overnight. Bradley and José express their desire to watch videos in the car since they do not get car sickness. However, Mac and Tyrone get car sick, so they opt out of the videos. On the drive, while Bradley and José watch videos, the others discuss the case.

Spencer closes his driver's door as his phone plays the tone for Agent Williams. He looks over at Mac, and his eye grows large as he answers. Ten minutes later, the team is on the road heading to Dayton, Ohio, for another fire. The agents are weary, and their body language confirms it. Everyone is speechless because they're all sharing the same feelings of dismay.

The weather progresses from sunshine to storms. By the time they arrive in Dayton, the sky sports low-hanging dark clouds with streaks of lightning and gusty winds. Rusty and Glenda Smellings are the owners of the latest gun store set on fire, and they sit in rocking chairs on the front porch of the store. After introductions, Rusty walks around with the guys giving a play-by-play of the events, while Mac stays back with Glenda. The fire did considerable damage to the rear of the building. It demolished the storage area and part of Rusty's gunsmithing area. The Dayton City Police contacted Rusty around three in the morning, advising him of the fire. A patrol officer spotted the fire while making rounds, and the officer also witnessed a guy wearing all black cut through the back of the lot toward the shopping center on the adjoining road. Spencer jots notes in his notebook for follow-up questions.

Rusty can produce surveillance video footage, but his logins are at his home office. He will send the info to Spencer for access. Tyrone receives permission to enter the structure for his own inspection. Inside the building, Tyrone instantly finds the evidence he needs. He brings out bits of melted plastic along with a partially burned shop rag. The fire-setter is relentless, if nothing else. All the gun store fires have started with Molotov cocktails using the same plastic gasoline cans and rags.

Spencer and the group ask Rusty and Glenda the same questions they asked the other owners. Neither one could remember a customer coming by the store eating Fritos. Nothing stands out but the police officer's description of the guy dressed in all black. They need to follow up with him. Mac suggests Rusty and Glenda move until they capture this guy, or at the very least for five days, assuming he'll move on by then. Rusty states he is not leaving his home, and he will hire his own security detail.

There is no arguing with Rusty, so the group bids them goodbye and drops in on the police department. They are in search of Officer Levonns. The desk sergeant advises the team that Officer Levonns will return tonight for his shift at seven. However, the sergeant, obviously taken by Mac, gives her the officer's cell phone number. He expresses his joy in helping an FBI agent by showing off his grin.

Spencer's guts twist as he watches the exchange between Mac and the sergeant. Mac didn't seem to notice or care about the sergeant's advances and his roaming eyes. She needs the phone number—that's all. Mac steps outside in the lobby and calls Office Levonns. He answers on the first ring and agrees to meet the group at a coffee shop down the street from the precinct.

While they wait for their coffee break, they drive to the adjoining shopping center. They want to see the fire-setter's escape route firsthand. This shopping plaza sits behind the gun store, and it faces a side street. Spencer parks the truck in the back of the lot. The group exits, and everyone walks around looking for evidence of a vehicle or a person. Mac finds the fire-setter to be a meticulous planner. This is an ideal location for a getaway vehicle. Trees separate the two buildings, and then more trees grow in the parking lot's landscaping pads. No one enters the front of the lot without being seen.

"Guys, this is the perfect spot to hide, with easy access to both roads and the target building. Now, I wonder about the fire-starters' background. These fires are premeditated down to the tiniest detail." Mac studies the area as she strolls around the lot and the tree line. "Another note of interest—the fires are happening in the wee hours of the morning, not late at night as the first ones. Few people work in their stores past midnight. Do you think the number of injured and dead concerns him?"

"I can only hope the death and injuries concern him. Otherwise, he is heartless," José' fumes and his tone causes the group to turn and look at him. "What? Why is everyone looking at me? Do you not agree?" José's neck vein protrudes from under the skin.

"We agree, José. We've just never heard you get angry. At least now we know you can get mad," Tyrone jokes.

As the group continues searching the grounds, nothing of interest pops. They decide to move to a hotel and work on the videos. Five videos remain, and they would like to knock them out tonight. No one knows what tomorrow will bring.

Some videos are lengthy, and Mac recognizes several of the same vehicles and trucks. It upset her she did not think of using the surrounding business cameras. They could have had these videos handled by now. Mac hates being behind in an investigation, and they started already behind in this one.

Morning arrives early with a call from the Dayton Police Department and Officer Levonns. He calls Spencer to explain the situation with the Smellings. Spencer rounds up the group for a ride to the Smellings' residence. "The fire-starter jumped a little early this time. He set fire to the Smellings' residence at 2:00 am. The security guard tried his best to put out the fire, but the heat was too close to the car when it exploded. The guard is in surgery to remove shrapnel from the explosion. His condition is unknown."

Tyrone speaks first. "That doesn't sound right unless the fire had been burning a while before the guard found it. How about the Smellings?"

Spencer states they are at the hospital with the guard. While turning out of the parking lot, a semi-truck cab passes the truck, going in the opposite direction. Spencer whips his head around to look at it again, but it's a blur. He ponders the idea of the semi-truck they spotted in the video. What are the chances the fire-starter drives it?

The crew arrives at the Smellings' residence to a ton of emergency responders. Officer Levonns greets them as they walk toward him. He shows them the damage to the back of the house. The house has a carport instead of a garage, which would explain the car explosion occurring so early in the fire. Rusty and Glenda sustained no injuries in the blaze. They heard the explosion and ran outside. Rusty notified the fire department, and since they are just half a mile down the street, they arrived on the scene within three minutes of the call. The officer confirms there were no other people in residence at the time of the fire and only one guard on duty.

Tyrone surveys the area around the origin of the fire but finds no evidence of Fritos. The car explosion destroyed all evidence. Tyrone wonders how many bags of Fritos it takes to start a fire of this size. He walks back to the group and explains the situation.

By the time the team returns to the hotel, it is breakfast time. Everyone is sleepy, but they refuse to give into it, so it's coffee and food. Mac asks Spencer, "Have you heard from Agent Williams about Jeremy's autopsy?"

"Not yet. I thought we would receive it yesterday, but I checked my email last night and nothing. Agent Williams did not email me at all yesterday, and I find that odd."

"That is odd. Now that I think back, I didn't get one either. Did he work yesterday?" Mac asks with a concerned look.

She picks up her phone and dials Agent Williams. The call routes to his voicemail. Mac then calls a coworker, "Stubin, it's Mac. I am trying to reach Agent Williams. Is he in the office? Yes, we are still tracking the arsonist."

The group watches Mac's face pale at the news. Once the call ends, Mac turns to face the guys and says, "Agent Williams's wife is in the hospital. The doctors diagnosed her with stage 4 breast cancer three weeks ago, and they are preparing for surgery. He is on a leave of absence. Stubin is filling in right now until we see what happens."

Spencer hugs Mac because he knows how close she is to Williams. Agent Williams is like a second dad to her. The other guys show sympathy to the group but are also consumed by their concerns with the case. "So, where does that leave us?" José asks the group.

Mac explains Agent Stubin has an exemplary record at the FBI, and nothing changes with the task force. It will continue as usual. Stubin will call them back once he reviews the case and sees where they are on it. Agent Williams notified the bureau this morning of his leave, so this is still a work in progress.

Bradley pipes in with, "We can work on the videos until we hear from Agent Stubin. We also need to follow up on the autopsy request. There would be no record of whether or not Agent Williams requested."

Thoughts of Agent Williams swirl through Mac's mind as she considers the last few days. The recent conversation she had with Agent Williams was brief. He seemed uninterested, but Mac did not question his mindset. His wife's condition might have been on his mind at the time. Mac wishes he would have shared with her about his wife. Everyone needs to share personal things with someone. Agent Williams always lends an ear to the team, and they should do the same for him.

Mac advises she is taking a walk. She needs fresh air before she sits in front of the laptop for hours. The guys agree, except they go up to their rooms. They make plans to meet in thirty minutes to begin on the videos.

After her time away, Mac is ready to tackle the next hurdle. Although she continues to worry about Agent Williams's wife, she will solve this case. The team will work through the videos and find this arsonist murderer. Mac sits in the small conference room off the lobby, waiting for the guys to emerge. She sips on coffee and shuffles her cards until she recognizes a pattern. The drive-by shooting and Jeremy's death are the trigger. Or could it be Jeremy's death is the trigger? So, the drive-by shooting caused Jeremy's death, and the result of death are the fires?

The guys enter the room with solemn expressions. But Mac jumps right in as she doesn't want to dwell on Agent Williams's situation. "I have another angle that I would like to discuss. I know I have mentioned the drive-by shooting is the trigger, but now I think it is Jeremy's death. Something ties the arsonist to Jeremy, and we need to find out what that it is."

Chapter 19

Silence ensues as the team ponders Mac's comments. Eyebrows raise, and heads bob as each member of the team works through the scenario. "Any idea what ties the two people together? The parents seem straight and narrow. His friends don't seem the kind to harbor grudges or start fires." Tyrone observes.

"I don't have a clue yet what the connection might be, but Jeremy and the arsonist must have one. Our job now is to find out what it is. When Stubin calls us, Jeremy's autopsy is first on my list. We need that today. Also, we've received no reports on Timmy Tanner."

Spencer agrees with Mac and moves to the table to start the videos. He received Rusty's account credentials, too, and they will begin with his videos. Although they don't expect to find that the fire-starter parked in the center behind the gun store, but they have to try.

The video begins, and they see nothing but a black screen. "Are we sure this is correct? I don't see any lights toward the parking lot." Bradley questions.

Just as he finishes, a flash of light appears in the center of the screen. It grows both in size and intensity. Then suddenly, it turns to the right, and the agent's gasp. They witness the dark-colored semi-truck turn right. It is the same truck as before, with no markings on the doors, no USDOT numbers, nothing. When the truck turns, the license plate is barely visible on one side.

Mac regains her composure. "Based on this video, our concentration focuses on finding this truck. The truck has been at two scenes for sure. Keep going and see if we can place him at more stores."

Tyrone asks Spencer if he can grab a still shot of the truck. They can use it as evidence collection because this is the best photo so far. Spencer complies and restarts the video. "Keep this one going in case he materializes again."

Thirty minutes later, the video ends without another visual of the truck. So, Spencer moves onto the fire in Ocala. With the video running toward the end, the same truck pops into view. This time, it rides by the store slowly in one direction, then a minute later, he rides by in the opposite direction. Spencer takes a print of this one, too. With the visual in Ocala, they now have three sightings of the same truck.

Lake City's video proves useless, as do the videos from Valdosta and Macon. Nashville adds a little flair to its video with an image of a man in a hoodie. Everyone jumps to attention when that image appears. Even with the picture, the guy is unidentifiable. They know he is Caucasian, but other than that, they have nothing. Only one more to go, and the videos will be complete.

An hour passes, and they have nothing to show for it, again. Mac stretches her arms and looks at her watch. "Guys, we have spent all day with the videos. At least we are current, and we have evidence placing the guy at the scenes of multiple fires."

Tyrone slips off to take a call from his wife. So, the others discuss the next step in the investigation. Without the autopsy and information on Timmy, they have no fresh leads. "How can we get ahead of this guy until we have more information? We can chase this guy forever at the rate we are moving." Mac throws the question out to the guys.

"Mac, we're all frustrated but other than notifying all gun store owners along the Interstate 75 corridor, there is not much else we can do," Spencer adds.

All eyes turn to him. "That is a great idea! I vote we make that happen today. Right now if we can. We should have considered this a long time ago." Bradley's energy is contagious, and the team is ecstatic. This move has the capability of demolishing the fire-starter's goals.

Tyrone places his cell in his pocket and walks over to the table. "What's with the commotion?"

"Spencer gave us the brilliant idea of notifying all gun store owners along the Interstate 75 corridor about the fires," Mac shares.

"Fantastic. Wouldn't it be something if a gun store owner captured this guy for us? How can we notify the owners in a timely fashion? It will take too long to do an internet search for individual towns. We are liable to miss one or two." Tyrone glances at Mac as he asks the questions.

"If Agent Williams was working, he could handle it for us. We'll try Agent Stubin. He can make calls for us, and the FBI can handle the notifications," Mac advises.

The team stands and prepares to leave the room when Mac's phone rings. She answers on the first ring as the caller ID reveals Stubin. Mac mouths to everyone, "Stubin," so they remain in the room with her. She listens to Stubin describe the traffic stop in which the police arrested Timmy Tanner. They picked Timmy up on a BOLO in South Georgia. He confessed to the shooting during his interrogation, saying he didn't intend for anyone to die. He aimed for the wall, but the bullet struck the guys instead because he didn't compensate for the moving vehicle. Timmy harbored a grudge over not making the basketball team, and his frustration got the best of him. Timmy confirmed Willie was his passenger and had nothing to do with the shooting.

After Stubin shares Timmy's story, Mac follows up on the request for Jeremy's autopsy. Stubin checked the request log, and there is no request. Fuming, Mac tries to calm her temper. She realizes it's not Stubin's fault, but they needed the report two days ago. Stubin enters the request as they speak. Next, Mac explains they want to notify all gun store owners along Interstate 75 about the arsonist. Stubin agrees and will handle the notifications from the Atlanta Field Office. He indicates Baxter is helping with the workload.

It relieved Mac when the call ends. Stubin was gracious and willing to do anything to help the team find this arson murderer. However, he asked them to stay in Dayton in case the fire-starter is rolling north. The group will be closer to the fire than being in Atlanta.

After her conversation with Stubin, Mac shares the details. The guys look deflated at the news of remaining in Dayton. Now, they will work on identifying the semi-truck. "Spencer, can you call a contact in the tech unit and have them work on the semi-truck's identity, and José or Bradley, can you do the same with your group?" Everyone nods in agreement.

Once they contact their respective tech groups, the team calls it a day and waits for answers. Mac advises the group she is eating in the hotel restaurant and then going to her room as she needs rest. The guys eat with her, but then slide over to the bar area. No one mentions the case. Their conversation centers on their families and who they have waiting at home for them. Almost four weeks away is a long time, and it is not over yet.

A night apart from the team is just what Mac needs. She relaxes in the tub with the hottest water her body can handle. As she soaks, the tension ebbs away while her mind gravitates to Spencer, because she is concerned something is changing in him. He acts preoccupied—like his mind is not in the game. Mac admits to herself she dislikes the changes. She can't live with someone who keeps secrets or lies. If she has a choice to keep him or not, the answer is not. Living with a cheater or liar is not for her.

After a restful night, Mac sits in the hotel restaurant eating a waffle and fruit and sipping coffee. Her mind and body rested. As she finishes her food, the guys stroll through the door. "Good morning, team. How was your night?' Mac asks with a grin.

The guy's grunt while walking to the buffet table. Mac snickers because she knows they enjoyed the bar last night. They'll pay for it until they get enough coffee and food. Tyrone is the first one to join Mac at the table. "Mac, you look well-rested this morning," Tyrone prods.

"I slept well for once, without the case keeping me awake, and I enjoyed my downtime. What about you?"

Tyrone swallows then replies, "I left the bar early and slept like a baby.
Who knows how late the others stayed at the bar. But from the grunts, it sounds like they stayed past their bedtime." Tyrone chuckles as he knows the troubles all too well.

When the rest of the team joins, Spencer inquires, "What are we doing today? We haven't received the autopsy to follow up on it. They arrested Timmy, and the tech units will call when they have something."

Bradley speaks first, "Our only outstanding issue is Simon Burden. No one at ATF has tracked him down. They found a guy in Switzerland who might be Simon, but we haven't heard from our Swiss counterparts yet."

"Switzerland? It sounds like Hunter went to a lot of trouble to involve this guy when he could have opened a Swiss bank about without him," Spencer comments.

The group runs through ideas on the Swiss information. No one has a response to it yet. Mac's cell rings, and she answers. She speaks with Stubin for a few minutes. Her shoulders sag when he shares the latest on the fire-setter, but she perks up at the end. The guys are eager for her to hang up so they can hear news.

"We should receive the autopsy by noon today. Our arsonist is in Detroit, Michigan. This time the good guys won! The store hired a security guard after receiving the FBI alert. The guard watched the arsonist walk to the back of the store with gallon jugs of gas. When the security guard confronted him, he hit the security guard with a full jug. Gas sprayed the guard in the face, and the arsonist sprinted away from the scene. The guard can only describe the guy as between 6' and 6'3", roughly 190 lbs with a limp. The good guys won this time! Stubin wants us to travel to Detroit to meet with the security guard who remains in the hospital." The last statement strikes a blow to the team.

"Why do we need to meet with this guard in person? You just said the guard could not ID the guy because of gas in his eyes. He even went to the ER for treatment, and they might admit him to the hospital, depending on the severity of the damage. Detroit is another few hours away, so we'd be that much further from Atlanta. I'll speak with Stubin and see if I can persuade him to let us skip this trip. We want to get back to Atlanta if nothing else, for Jeremy's autopsy," Spencer retorts.

The team glances between Spencer and Mac, not knowing how to respond. Spencer rarely bounces back at Mac in that manner. Mac helps the guys, "Call him. I am all for driving back to Atlanta. We can do a phone interview with the guard just as easily." She sits back and waits for the guys to finish their meal. Then Spencer excuses himself from the table and steps outside to make the call to Stubin.

Thirty minutes pass as the team watches Spencer pace around the parking lot, talking with Stubin. Finally, Spencer returns to the table. "Here's where we stand. We are driving to Atlanta today. I convinced Stubin there is nothing to see in Detroit. No fire damage to the building, and the guard can't ID the arsonist. We will conduct a phone interview with the guard in the next day or two. He's in the hospital with burns on his face and hands. His recovery time is a week or so. With no surgery and minimal scars, the guard is lucky. Agent Williams's wife is undergoing breast surgery tomorrow at Emory. Stubin shared Williams doesn't want us to worry and keep working, but I know Mac will want to sit by his side all day. So, the final answer is that we are going to Atlanta. Meet at the truck in thirty minutes."

Twenty minutes later, the team converges on the truck. Eager to return to Atlanta, they load the truck quickly. The sunshine is bright as they drive into it. No one talks as they send text messages to home and work counterparts. The drive's first hours are quiet. Then the guys perk up as they get closer to Atlanta. Mac thinks of Agent Williams and what he must go through. He has been married to the same woman for forty-five years. In today's time, that's an accomplishment. Tha's the kind of marriage Mac strives for herself.

Lunch is in a fast-food eatery just over the Tennessee border. Traffic has been on their side today. Mac's phone rings during the meal. She takes the call outside since it is Stubin, and he advises her to check her email for the autopsy report. Mac takes her place at the table and shares the news with the guys. She wants to read it. There is some connection between Jeremy and the fire-starter, and this could verify that for them.

Stubin is correct; the results are in, and Mac clicks the email to open it. She peruses the document slowly because she wants to overlook nothing. The coroner describes Jeremy's injuries from the gunshot. The bullet struck the collarbone, then tore through his body, causing extreme damage to multiple vital organs. There would have been no way to save Jeremy unless he had immediate access to an operating room and a team of surgeons to stem the blood flow.

The coroner's report mentions Jeremy's kidney appears older than his age. Jeremy had only one working kidney at the time of death. Also noted is the left kidney rests on the right side of the body just in case Jeremy required further surgeries. Which Mac discovers is a typical move for doctors if they fear additional surgery, is a possibility.

After her review, Mac shares the results with the team. "The only reason for a kidney to be older than its owner is a transplant. Right?" Tyrone questions the team.

Mac confirms the toxicology levels show immunosuppressant drugs in the blood, which would indicate a transplant, too. The kidney is the only organ mentioned in the report.

Everyone works through the information, then agrees with Tyrone. Now, they need to track down Jeremy's doctors to determine the cause of the older kidney. Mac grimaces when she realizes she must deal with Jeremy's parents again. They are the saddest couple, and that kind of sadness seeps into Mac's bones, and it takes days to diminish. Spencer watches Mac's face as she considers speaking with the couple again. Stepping up for Mac, Spencer agrees to make this phone call at the next stop. They will stop for gas shortly, and he can call them for the information.

Now, she prays they divulge the doctor's contact information to Spencer. Since the police notified them of Jeremy's killer, their case is closed. Spencer must convey the relevance of this information. He must also stress that the information he shares is not public knowledge.

"Fingers crossed. I'm calling Jeremy's parents while one of you pumps our gas," Spencer explains as he exits the truck. He looks around the lot and ambles over to a picnic area. The group watches as he punches the number, and his mouth moves. While José pumps the gas, the others go into the store for a break. Before their purchases are complete, Spencer walks in the door with a thumbs up. He has the doctor's information. The team shares a fist bump on the way to the truck.

"Also, I called the doctor's office and left a message for him. He is seeing patients this afternoon. So, we wait again."

Mac checks her phone for messages and finds nothing. She has not heard from her dad for several days. Quickly, she sends a text requesting a health update. The last she heard, her dad's health improved, but she still likes to hear from him.

Arriving in Atlanta during rush-hour traffic is nerve-wracking. It takes two hours to get through the downtown connector in stop-and-go traffic. Just as Spencer is about to exit, his phone rings. The group listens to the conversation. Jeremy's doctor is on the line, and Spencer extends the request regarding Jeremy's medical records. He shares his thoughts on Jeremy's older kidney. The doctor hesitates before answering, but paints a picture for the group.

As a young child, Jeremy was sick with hereditary kidney disease. He spent a lot of time in a hospital bed. Since his adoption, the family sought a donor from outside the family. The doctor recites information on kidney donation that the group knew nothing about. He explains that living kidney donors can be up to thirty years older than the recipient if their kidneys are in excellent shape. Blood type is a significant concern with organ transplants, and the Kinds were no match. The doctor referred them to Jeremy's transplant doctor to get the donor's information and advised them to get a warrant.

Once the conversation ends, everyone lets out a sigh. "Well, that confirms the transplant, but who is the donor, and is the donor our arsonist?" Mac contemplates.

Each step in the investigation gets them one step closer to the finish line. But with mighty small steps, it takes a long time. The group breaks when they reach the parking lot as each member runs for their own vehicle. No one stops by the office before leaving for home. Mac calls her parents as she drives toward their house for a brief visit, then she will head home. Tomorrow, she plans on sitting with Agent Williams while his wife is in surgery, unless a fire gets in her way.

Chapter 20

Mac walks into the surgery waiting room at 7:00 am. Agent Williams sits alone, nursing a cup of coffee. He appears ragged when he makes eye contact with Mac. "Hi, Williams. I am joining you for a few hours of downtime." Mac pauses, then adds, "Why didn't you tell us about your wife? You don't have to go through this alone." Mac takes the seat beside him and settles in for a long wait.

"I want you and Spencer to finish this investigation. I would have told you after the surgery, but it all happened so fast. We thought we would have to wait for surgery until next month, but there was an opening, and we took it. The kids are not even here yet. One is traveling here today, and the other is not traveling until tomorrow. They're not happy with the situation either, but neither of us like waiting. A dark cloud looms over a person waiting for a serious operation, knowing cancer is growing inside daily." Williams touches his eyes with a tissue. Mac has never seen him emotional before, and it tugs at her heartstrings.

"No one can blame either of you for wanting to get the surgery behind you. Everything will be fine, and things will get back to normal." Mac pats his arm like she does her dad and sits back in a chair.

"Thanks for coming, Mac. I appreciate it. Now, tell me about the investigation. It will take my mind off things for a little while, anyway."

Mac and Agent Williams discuss every fire, injury, and death. Agent Williams can't believe the arsonist is still going strong after all this time. He suspects he will eventually make a mistake and bring attention to himself.

Also, Mac confirms Timmy Tanner is the shooter, and Willie is no longer in custody. Willie agrees to testify in court that Timmy is the shooter if it comes to that. With Timmy's confession, we might not have a trial for the shooting after all.

When Mac explains about the transplant, Agent Williams's eyes grow wide, and his mouth opens. "How on earth did you discover the transplant information?"

"I always say crimes begin with a trigger and a connection. Once I found the trigger, we searched for the link. We also have photos of the same semi-truck at several fires, but the truck has no identifiable markings. The FBI and ATF tech units are assisting with the truck.

Agent Williams explores the idea that the donor is the arsonist. He glances at Mac for her thoughts, and her grin says it all. "You agree with me, right? Otherwise, you wouldn't be grinning like that."

"Absolutely, I do. That is the connection. I surmise the kidney donor started setting fires to gun stores when Hunter Bows' name appeared in the newspaper article. It just so happened the donor read it and took things into his own hands. Now, the question is, would the donor have started fires anyway without knowing Hunter Bows' name? That is something we may never know."

Spencer walks through the door and enters with cups of coffee. "Can I join the party, or am I too late?"

Agent Williams stands to greet Spencer. "Thanks for coming, but you didn't have to unless you have information on the case. Mac shared the information you all have gathered."

"The only recent information is that I called the transplant coordinator and supplied her with the warrant she needs to release the donor information. We should have the donor's name by the end of the business day," Spencer explains.

Mac speculates on the turns their case will take with this information. The threesome sits as the clock ticks above their heads. Mac stands and walks around the waiting room as she tries to get her blood flowing. The view from the window is awful as it just looks at another medical building. Hopefully, Mrs. Williams's surgery is a success. This has been a sad case from the start, and they need something to lift their spirits.

After four hours, the doctor walks into the waiting room and speaks with Agent Williams. With the surgery a success, Mrs. Williams is in recovery and will remain there for two hours. He suggests Agent Williams eat lunch while she is in recovery and once she is out, he can visit with her.

Lunch at the hospital cafeteria turns out to be delicious. One section of the buffet is southern cooking, and Mac grabs a little of everything. Her plate holds fried chicken, macaroni and cheese, turnip greens, and black-eyed peas. Of course, she could not forget the cornbread and sweet tea. Agent

Williams and Spencer watch her consume the plate of food in awe.

"Mac, I've never seen you eat so much food. You must have been famished," Agent Williams states as Mac takes a sip of sweet tea.

"No sir, not famished, but I don't get southern cooking often, and when I do, I eat it. This food is delicious. It tastes like Mom's cooking—or close to it. When I was growing up, this is the way she cooked dinner every night. My brothers and I would sit around the table together, eat, and tell our parents about our day."

Mac glances at Spencer as he finishes up his grilled chicken salad and chuckles. "How was your salad, Spencer?"

"Delicious, just as you said. I can't figure where you put all that food." Spencer places his napkin on the table and sits back, enjoying the atmosphere. The sun shines through the window and casts a glow around Mac's face. He notices her carefree beauty, and the pit of his stomach flutters. Love is a strange thing.

After lunch, Mac and Spencer escort Agent Williams back to the waiting room for his chance to see his wife. The duo leaves and promises to check in later on Mrs. Williams and give a case update.

Spencer and Mac follow in tandem to the FBI office in Atlanta. Stubin insists on meeting them for an update on the case. As they flash their credentials at the door, Spencer's phone rings. He pulls it from his pants pockets and motions for Mac to join him. They hurry to a quiet corner of the lobby while Spencer addresses the caller. His face is a myriad of emotions, finally settling on surprise. "You will not believe who the donor is?"

"Tell me, Spencer. Who is it?" Mac fidgets, waiting on Spencer's reply.

"The donor is Gilbert Broth. He's Bobby's dad, right?"

"That is a bombshell I didn't see coming. Gilbert Broth is Jeremy's kidney donor. I didn't ask him about employment, because Gilbert never entered my mind as a suspect. My questions related to Jeremy and the shooting. Do you think he's a truck driver?" Mac asks.

Spencer shakes his head in disbelief and says, "Anything is possible with this case. None of us considered Bobby's dad could be the arsonist. We need to share this newsflash with Stubin, and then we will make the call to Bobby."

The elevator ride is quiet. Mac works her puzzle pieces to satisfy the case. But Bobby's dad never came into question. How can that be? Gilbert was at the shooting scene, but they never questioned him about the possibility of being an arsonist. Mac's insides quiver when she realizes they overlooked him as a suspect.

Stubin directs the duo to the chairs in front of his desk. Once seated, Spencer shares the latest news. No one suspected Gilbert Broth of anything, especially the fires. Stubin advises he read the case file, and he agrees with the team. Nothing points to Gilbert Broth. He suggests Mac call Bobby and find out more about his dad. Stubin references the file when he reminds the duo that Bobby is not close with his dad.

While Mac walks to her desk, she conjures up questions to ask Bobby. She needs to know about Gilbert's past, if he was in the Army, and where he currently works. Bobby is the more fragile of the two friends, and she doesn't want to jeopardize their relationship further until she gets answers.

Mac's mouth is dry as she finds Bobby in her contacts. This call can make or break this case, and it rests in Mac's hand. She must handle this call cautiously. The team is ready to end this nonsense of fires and murders. Mac grasps how vital this call is to the case. She takes several deep breaths to calm her nerves.

Bobby's phone rings five times, and then his voicemail answers. Mac leaves her name and number but offers no reason for the call. Her concentration wavers as she handles emails and glances at her phone, willing it to ring. Stubin calls on her office phone, asking for a status on Gilbert. Mac relays her account, and they wait.

As time crawls, Mac revisits the case material, beginning with Gilbert's interview. It was a short one, and he explained how he treated Jeremy and Bobby at the scene. Other than that, he offered nothing. He failed to mention he gave Jeremy a kidney, although I am not sure it would have meant much to the team at the time. Once Mac satisfies herself with the review, she walks to the coffee bar. Why hasn't Bobby returned her call? Does Gilbert know they are onto him?

Mac turns a corner, heading toward her desk when she spots Spencer leaning against a column.

He speaks in a hushed tone with someone on the phone, and the other person sounds upset. Not that Mac eavesdrops on other people's calls, but she is interested in this one. She hasn't noticed Spencer receiving odd calls lately, but that doesn't mean he's stopped receiving them either.

She slides up behind him and wraps her arm around his waist. When he turns and sees Mac, his phone drops out of his hand, and he clambers to the floor to grab it. "What on earth did you do that for, Mac?" Spencer questions in a brief tone.

"I didn't know you would drop your phone. Did I scare you that bad? You could call them back if the call dropped." Mac bends over to retrieve Spencer's phone, but he beats her to it, almost knocking her over. "Oh, I see. Another secret phone call," she spits out and stomps off.

Furious, Mac goes to the ladies' room so Spencer can't follow. She stews over their confrontation. Why is he hiding phone calls? He tells her not to worry and to trust him, but how much more of this craziness can she take? After the case, and once Agent Williams returns, she will request a new partner. The change will be good for both of them. Mac gathers herself together and peeks out the door to make sure no one is standing outside. The hallway is clear, but unfortunately Spencer sits in her chair.

"Why are you sitting in my chair when yours is empty?" Mac snaps.

"I need to apologize to you, and I couldn't follow you into the ladies' room. My mom called crying about my sister, and I was trying to listen to her when you startled me."

"I'm the one who's sorry. The way you responded, I assumed it was another secret phone call. Now, what is wrong with your sister? Is she okay?" Mac backs down, feeling awful for her outburst.

"My sister, Emily, lives in Savannah and suffered injuries in a car wreck. She is en route to the trauma center. Mom is frantic. I called the trauma center for word on her condition. I'm not leaving here until I find out the seriousness. Sometimes Mom exaggerates, and I don't want to jump to conclusions. As soon as they call, I'll know more."

"Emily is your younger sister, right? I sure hope she is okay. What happened in the wreck?" Mac inquires.

"All mom knows is Emily was a front-seat passenger riding with her boyfriend. A truck failed to yield at an intersection, and it struck her boyfriend's car on the driver's side, throwing the car across the road into a ditch. We don't know her boyfriend's condition either."

"Why don't you make your way to your mom's house, just in case? You need to check on her, anyway. I'll stay here until I get in touch with Bobby, and then we can see where we are." Mac can't believe he wasn't on his way home to be with his mom. Her family jumps when any of them have issues. He sits quietly for a few minutes before agreeing with Mac.

Spencer walks out of the office door, calling his mom. Mac hears him explain to her he is on his way and to calm down. Mac's gut clenches at the despair Spencer's mom must be feeling. Here is another mom getting the dreaded phone call that something terrible has happened to her child. It must be nothing short of devastating, especially when the child is in another city. Mac is glad her family lives close enough they are reachable if something terrible happens.

Mac is walking toward Stubin's office to share Spencer's predicament when her phone rings. Assuming it's Spencer, she doesn't check the caller ID. Mac stammers when Bobby is the caller. Her notes are on her desk on the other side of the building. She makes small talk while trotting back to her office. Bobby asks if there is news on Jeremy's murder. Surprised at the question, Mac advises they arrested the murderer several days ago. Now, Bobby grows suspicious of the phone call and goes silent. Mac calms her nerves, hoping to squelch his anxiety.

Bobby answers Mac's questions about his dad, but he pauses toward the end of the interrogation. He admits to not thinking about the kidney transplant since it was over five years ago. Finally, he's had enough, and he asks Mac why all the questions. Mac explains their concerns with the kidney transplant and the fires.

"So, let me get this straight. You and your team of agents think my dad is the arsonist. That is the craziest thing I've heard! Yes, Dad drives a truck part time, and yes, he was in the Army, but he has had no run-ins with the law, ever. Since the divorce from my mom, he lives alone, and he's only dated a few people. He mainly keeps to himself. I can't imagine Dad doing anything like this because Jeremy died. When he found out, he would be a donor, he seemed happy. Dad felt he was doing something worthwhile. Since he got out of the Army, he says his life isn't full, and he feels lost. He followed up with Jeremy weekly for a while after the surgery. Once he thought Jeremy would make it with his kidney, his calls were fewer because he didn't want to annoy Jeremy." Bobby sniffs.

"Why does your dad only drive trucks occasionally?" Mac continued with the questions.

"While in the Army, an IED caused him a significant injury, and the Army medically discharged him. The blast mangled his left leg, and he walks with a limp. Long-distance driving makes the leg hurt," Bobby answers.

Mac pauses before asking the last question. "Bobby, do you know where your dad is right now? We'd like to speak to him."

"I don't. We really don't have a lot in common and only talk every so often. I would like to call him first," Mac hears Bobby sniff, knowing tears are falling. Not only did Bobby lose a best friend in Jeremy, but he might also lose his dad, too. Mac hopes he is strong enough to pick up the pieces and keep going. Life is hard enough without these extra trials. Mac reluctantly agrees to let Bobby call his dad first, but she worries she might regret that later.

After the call, Mac trots to Stubin's office. She waits at his door while he finishes up a call and peeks in the office when she hears the phone hit the cradle. "Do you have time for updates?"

Stubin raises his eyebrows, "Did you say updates as in plural?"

Mac explains Spencer's issue with his sister and his mom. Stubin writes a note in his book with no expression. Next, she shares her conversation with Bobby Broth, the kidney donor's son, and Stubin leans back in his chair after she finishes.

"Based on what we know, do you think Gilbert Broth is our arsonist?" Stubin looks Mac in the eye as he asks.

"Yes, I do. Gilbert fits the profile. I don't agree with Bobby about Gilbert driving only on occasion. I think he drives often, or at least he does now. Bobby didn't mention any issues with fires in the past, so I can't explain why Gilbert decided to start setting fires. Maybe something he's watched on the TV or searched on the internet. Who knows?"

"Bring Gilbert Broth in for interrogation. I'll start on the warrant now since we need to find him first before interrogating him. With Spencer out, you will pair with Baxter. Let the other members of the team know as well. Keep me updated. Thanks, Mac."

Chapter 21

Priorities are brutal at times like these when there are so many, it's hard to figure out which should be on top. Should Mac call Spencer first, or maybe Agent Williams, or what about Baxter? Mac likes Baxter, but now is not the time to learn a new partner. She'll move forward without him if she must. Spencer and his sister's situation cross her mind. Then Agent Williams comes to mind, and Mac pushes everything to the back and turns her attention to the case.

Gilbert Broth is the suspected arsonist murderer. His name never came up in team discussions as a suspect. Why should it? Gilbert attempted to save Jeremy's life by tying a tourniquet over his wounds. Would a regular person tie a tourniquet over a massive wound at the shoulder area? Mac believes no, they would not, only someone not afraid of injuries, like an Army veteran. She places a call to Stubin with a request. "Can you get me Gilbert Broth's Army record? I want to know what kind of person we are dealing with here, particularly his injuries."

Mac ends the call and arranges the files on her desk in order of priority. Bobby hasn't called with an update on his dad, and that is worrisome. Mac dials Bobby and receives his voicemail. She promised Bobby she would not call Gilbert first, but how much longer can she wait? Bobby has two more hours, and then she will contact Gilbert herself. Then she remembers she didn't pry the number out of Bobby. While she was on the phone with Bobby, she should have insisted he give her the number before letting him off the phone. He tugged at her heart of how he spoke about his dad, and she hadn't pushed the topic. Now, it will be her fault if Bobby doesn't come through.

Baxter has not shown up yet, so Mac calls Agent Williams for an update on his wife. He answers, and his voice sounds relieved. They discussed Mrs. Williams's surgery and recovery. The doctors say they found no cancer cells in the lymph nodes when they tested them after the mastectomy. So, after the hospital stay, they expect that Mrs. Williams will make a full recovery. There has been no talk about reconstructive surgery yet. Agent Williams defers to his wife on that topic. He hopes to be back at work in two weeks. He wants his wife to be mobile before he leaves her home alone. Agent Williams expresses his concern for Gilbert Broth. Mac states they will capture him soon. Their conversation ends when the nurse enters to check Mrs. Williams's vitals.

Mac hears a noise in the hall and knows it is Baxter. He has never been subtle a day in his life. "Hey, Mac. I hear we're working together while Spencer is away. I've read the reports on the fires. What is the team working on today?"

"Uh, well, I have not called them yet. Let me make a few quick calls, then we'll meet to discuss the most recent discoveries. Give me fifteen minutes." Mac grabs her phone and starts dialing. She can't believe she didn't begin with them. They need to know the latest information, too. Baxter sits in front of her desk the entire time she calls the team. She gives them a synopsis and advises the group about a 9:00 am meeting in the office.

Baxter takes notes, and his first question grates on Mac's nerves. "Do you have Gilbert's phone number? We can call him or even ping his phone to find his location."

Now, Mac is chastising herself again for not getting the number. How careless can she be? The cell locator never entered her mind while she spoke with Bobby. "I don't have it. Bobby, Gilbert's son, asked to contact his dad first. I gave him until 6:00 pm. I left a message on Bobby's voicemail earlier requesting an update, but he hasn't returned my call."

"You realize he might not call you back, right? Then, how can we find Gilbert's number? We can't ID him from the pictures of his truck. Stubin is waiting for his Army record, but that will not give us a phone number. I can't believe you, of all people, didn't make Bobby give you his dad's number." Baxter scolds with contempt as his eyes bore holes into Mac's.

Baxter has never spoken to her in this manner. Mac gathers her wits. "What's gotten into you, Baxter? I know exactly what I did and why I did it. Can you tell me all your decisions have been perfect? Let me answer for you—no. You can't. I have faith in Bobby to come through. It may not be in my time or yours, but he will come through. He wants to see this thing finished too. Why don't you head home and come back in the morning for the team meeting? I will handle things tonight. If anything transpires, I'll call." Mac grabs her phone and dials a number, giving Baxter the excuse to leave. He takes it, and Mac's tension subsides as she returns the phone to the cradle.

After Baxter's escape, Mac tries to reason with Baxter's response to the phone number. She's never seen him act the way he did today. Is something bothering him, too?

When Mac's phone rings, she jumps. She is studying her cards again, and nothing points to Gilbert as a suspect. Spencer calls and gives a brief update on his sister. He drove his mom to Savannah so she could be with her. His mom is calmer now that they are together. The accident was horrific by Spencer's account. A police officer from the traffic reconstruction team dropped by the hospital to check on her and her boyfriend for the report. The boyfriend is in critical condition with multiple fractures in his left leg, while Spencer's sister received many contusions and a few airbag burns. In time, she will make a full recovery. However, Spencer is not sure about the boyfriend. He has a second surgery scheduled tonight. If they can save his leg, he will be one lucky kid. The police officer charged the other driver with a dozen infractions, and he is in the ICU, too. If the boyfriend doesn't make it, they will add vehicular manslaughter to the charges.

After Spencer updates Mac on his sister, he asks about the case. "Stubin assigned Baxter to me since you are out, and that's not working out too good so far. I'm hoping he cools down before he speaks to me again," Mac offers.

"What did he say to you?" Heat rises in Spencer's gut. "If he misbehaves, I want to know." Spencer feels his blood pressure rise to the boiling point.

"We'll discuss it when you get back. Nothing to worry about now. I handled myself rather well." Mac discusses the recent events, and they are in wait mode for Bobby to call. Spencer agrees with Mac that Bobby will do what he said. Bobby admitted to not having a close relationship with his father. It might take longer than a few hours before Bobby can get in touch with him. Spencer even said it might be tomorrow before he calls. Mac settles down after speaking with Spencer and looks forward to his arrival back home sometime tomorrow. His mom will stay with his sister while she recuperates at home.

Stubin enters Mac's office and suggests she go home. There is nothing to do tonight. He instructs her to call if she hears from Bobby, no matter the time. Mac obliges and shuts down her computer and walks to the elevator for the ride down.

Mac drives home in a stupor. She feels disappointed because she has not heard from Bobby. Her instincts might have let the team down. They haven't received notice of another fire since Detroit. Maybe that debacle scared Gilbert enough to stop the arsons. If that is so, they will never capture him if he high-tails it out of Georgia, and that will haunt Mac forever. Whether federal or local, every investigator will have one case that gets away sometime in their career. Mac doesn't want this one to be the one that got away.

Mac's night is routine for her. She catches up on laundry, does a few household chores, and talks with her mom and dad. She goes to bed early to read her book. However, she falls asleep with the book lying on her chest. The sound of her ringing cell phone startles her from sleep. She grabs it from her nightstand and answers. The caller is Bobby, and the call is brief. With her nerves rattled, she calls Stubin.

"Stubin, it's Mac. I just heard from Bobby. In a frantic voice, he told me to be at a Chattanooga, Tennessee, gun store tomorrow night on Interstate 24 at Exit 2. I asked him why, and he said just do it and call him back afterward. All I can figure is his dad will be there."

"That's what it sounds like. We'll discuss plans at the team meeting. Try to rest, and I'll see you there." Stubin ends the call, and Mac figures he is probably asleep again soon.

Mac, on the other hand, can't sleep now. She replays Bobby's call and the way his voice sounded. He is frantic about his father. Mac walks around her apartment, searching for things to do to take her mind off Bobby. Spencer would want to know about Bobby. So she picks up her phone but remembers it is the middle of the night. She lays her phone down on her nightstand, picks up her book, and reads. The last time she sees the clock, it reads 3:30 am.

With her alarm blaring, Mac snatches her phone from the nightstand. She squints while reading the clock, wishing she can roll over for another hour or two of sleep. There is no way she can miss this team meeting. She dresses in record time and drives to the office. The sunshine beats its way into the windshield, making driving difficult. Mac glances at her phone and notices a missed call from Spencer. She taps his number. He answers on the first ring.

His voice sounds so good this morning. After yesterday, this day can only be better. "Good morning, Spencer. Are you driving?"

"Yes, I'm driving. I am on my way back to Atlanta since my mom and sister are settled. My sister will be in the hospital for two or three days while they treat the burns. Mom is staying in Savannah while my sister recuperates. I'll return to Savannah to bring mom home in a few weeks. Now, what are you doing this morning?" Spencer asks.

Mac explains the events of last night with Bobby's call as Spencer listens intently. He asks a few clarifying questions, and he is glad to be coming home. He wants to be a part of the takedown team tonight in Chattanooga. He will be at the Atlanta field office by noon. Spencer asks Mac to include him in the team meeting by speakerphone.

With high spirits, Mac enters the FBI field office, eager to begin the team briefing. She has several items to pass along and knowing Spencer will be here by noon makes it easier. Stubin stops Mac as soon as she steps off the elevator. He emailed Gilbert's Army record. Her heart flutters with anticipation. "Great. I'll see if I can glean anything from it before our meeting." She settles into her chair then opens the email, as it is the first one in her inbox.

She reads it line by line. Gilbert Broth, birthdate, last known address, divorced, lists Bobby as an only child. Not much to the report until she gets to the bottom. Gilbert was an Army lifer. He pledged to retire from the Army until his Humvee rode over an IED. The blast decimated his unit. Gilbert was the lucky one, sustaining only a left leg injury. His injury required multiple surgeries and several blood transfusions. One other unit member is in a vegetative state in a German hospital. The rest of his team died in the desert. The military diagnosed Gilbert with a severe case of PTSD, and he takes daily medication. He has not been in any trouble with the law—not even a speeding ticket—since he returned to the states.

Mac leans back in her chair and contemplates Gilbert's actions. The only conclusion is Jeremy's death triggered Gilbert's PTSD. The combination sparked a hatred for gun stores, especially Hunter Bows's store. Once he started setting the fires, he could not stop, not even when death occurred. Mac can't explain the fires—maybe Gilbert thought that would make a more dramatic scene? Then Mac realizes he will probably plead insanity, but he will be off the street, nonetheless.

With the minutes ticking away, Mac readies herself to present the most recent information. Now, she will add Gilbert's Army career to the meeting. Her team members sit around the conference room table, talking with Stubin as Mac enters. She exchanges pleasantries with the group before dialing Spencer. The team is glad to know Spencer will be with them in Chattanooga. Now that Spencer can take part in the meeting, Mac begins.

She starts with Jeremy's autopsy results. The autopsy highlighted Jeremy's older kidney and immunosuppressants in the bloodstream. This information led Mac and Spencer to consider a connection to the donor. They spoke with Jeremy's doctors and confirmed he was a kidney recipient five years ago. Then, with the doctor's help in locating the transplant coordinator, they confirmed Bobby's dad, Gilbert Broth, was Jeremy's kidney donor.

Gilbert's Army career is a topic of discussion amongst the team, and everyone agrees with Mac. The mix of PTSD and Jeremy's death was the trigger that set him off. But no one can explain the fires. There is nothing in his file that would suggest he is a firebug.

Mac describes her call with Bobby, his panic, and his advice to be at a Chattanooga gun store that sits off Interstate 24W at Exit 2. Bobby didn't mention the time. In his haste, he said just to be there. She advises she has called Bobby several times, but he has not answered. Mac states, "So, we will be there from dusk until dawn, if that's what it takes. Spencer will be in the office around noon. We will meet again at two to review the plans. Questions?"

Everyone shakes their heads no and leaves the room. Spencer speaks to Mac. "Help me prepare the stakeout. See if you can find a satellite image of the gun store and surrounding buildings. Gilbert will hide his truck for easy access to the interstate. We need to know where that is. Also, notify the gun store owner. They need not be there."

"The information will be on your desk." Mac ends the call and begins on her tasks.

The satellite imagery turns out to be the hardest to accomplish. There are several images, but not one shows the entire building with the surrounding areas. Mac uses three images for their purpose. They have a building picture showing the parking lot with the road access directly to the interstate and the surrounding centers. Surveillance at this store will be tricky. The building's front is open from the main road, one side butts up to a hill, and the two remaining sides are open. The back is for deliveries, with the distance from the lot to the tree line being minimal.

Spencer's time in the FBI SWAT team will help prepare the group for tonight's surveillance. Baxter will join the group as an extra hand. So, that leaves Mac to notify the gun store owner and the local police.

Once she completes her tasks, Mac breaks for lunch. Bobby has not returned her calls, and she thinks she has gotten all the help she will get from Bobby until this is over. The situation between Bobby and his dad twists her heartstrings every time she thinks of it.

Spencer arrives at the FBI field office ten minutes past the hour in wrinkled clothes and a two-day-old beard. Between traveling and his sister's situation, he is absolutely exhausted. However, he develops a surveillance plan for tonight in record time. This type of assignment is second nature to Spencer, so it doesn't take much effort on his part. With the local police and the gun store owner notified, he is ready to reveal his plan during the afternoon meeting.

Mac peeks her head in Spencer's office just as he is completing his plans. "How is the plan coming along?"

"It is official. With that complete, I need a coffee. Care to join me?" Spencer motions to the door. He pecks her on the cheek as she passes him in the doorway.

"I'm glad you're back. For more reasons than work, but I wouldn't want to do the stakeout tonight without you." Mac's eyes meet Spencer's.

Spencer pushes the down button for the elevator. "I know what you mean. This has been a long, hard case, and we both deserve closure on it."

Stubin joins the duo for the coffee break, much to their dismay. He discusses the plan for tonight, and he advises he will be present for the stakeout and not in a leadership role. Stubin sees no issue with Spencer's plan and has high regard for its potential results. He is like the rest of the team, ready to get this one finished.

The team reconvenes in the conference room. Spencer explains considerably the plan. Each team member has a job and a pre-assigned location for the surveillance. After the meeting, no one asks follow-up questions of Spencer. Everyone will meet at dark near the site and then arrive separately to avoid converging on the store at the same time.

All members will wear black with their respective insignias printed on their ballistic vest or jacket. There will be teams of two, and no one is to approach Gilbert alone. When two approach him, two more will surround him from behind. The local police will monitor the roads in case Gilbert escapes capture. The fire department and EMS will stand by, too. All members will wear ear comms for communication. As Spencer nears the end, Baxter asks, "Are we sure Gilbert will make a move in this store tonight?"

Spencer glares at Baxter, aware of his comments to Mac. "Yes, we are sure. Bobby confirmed this in a call to Mac." Spencer's irritation with Baxter is obvious. His neck veins protrude as he speaks. "Baxter, I'm not sure what your problem is with this case, but we can handle it without your help. We don't need anyone who is less than 100% committed on the stakeout team."

Baxter, not wanting to upset Spencer further, apologizes, "Hey, man. I'm sorry. I meant nothing to it. If you let me, I'll be there." Baxter turns his eyes down and shrinks into his chair.

Stubin clears the air because of the comments between Spencer and Baxter. The meeting adjourns, with Stubin requesting a word with Baxter behind closed doors. Baxter concerns Stubin because he collides with everyone over everything. In the past, he got along well with the other agents. Something has caused changes in Baxter's demeanor, and Stubin needs an answer. He can't let Baxter be a part of this team if he tries to sabotage it at every step. First, it was with Mac, now with Spencer.

As Stubin walks to his office, he considers the job and how glad he will be when Agent Williams returns. Now he understands why he never put in for the Special Agent in Charge position of an office.

Mac watches as the two men walk into Stubin's office. "Wonder what is up with Baxter? He never acted like this before. Stubin and Baxter worked well together on the Drake case."

Spencer pauses before answering. "Baxter could have issues at home, for all we know. I have never seen him so combative before. Baxter and Stubin are close. Surely he will not unload on Stubin."

The group inspects their gear and tests the ear comms before stowing them away. Spencer briefs each team member individually and confirms their assignments. The only question from the team members concerns Baxter and his loyalty. No team wants a rogue member. Spencer informs the group of Stubin's relationship with Baxter, and if Baxter decides against partaking in tonight's surveillance, someone else can fill his shoes.

Mac watches the exchange with Spencer, and the teams take their respective gear and load it into a truck. Four black Suburban's sit packed and ready for the trip north. Now, they get to eat and rest. Tonight will be long since they have no idea what time Gilbert will show. Mac and Spencer review the fire cases, and none of the fires began before ten. The rendezvous time is eight, with the first check-in via the ear comms scheduled for 8:30 and another one every thirty minutes after that.

As Spencer and Mac exit the building, Stubin calls Spencer and advises Baxter will be his partner tonight. Stubin's voice carries a strange tone, so Spencer doesn't question his decision. Spencer's primary concern is Stubin allowing Baxter to be a part of the stakeout team just because of their friendship. Bad things happen when friendship impedes making a hard decision.

The evening progresses slowly for Mac. Her anticipation is contagious, and neither she nor Spencer can sleep. Mac speaks first. "Are you ready to drive north? I can't sit here anymore."

Chapter 22

"We'll get there early, but as you say, it's better to be early than late," Spencer states as he rises from his chair. They climb into the truck and drive north on Interstate 75. The traffic is somewhat decent for a change. Once they clear the city, the roadway opens, and they are clear all the way to Chattanooga. When they arrive, they realize they were not the first. Tyrone and his Atlanta PD partner, Paul, sit in their designated spot.

The others arrive on time, too. One hurdle complete. Spencer reviews the aerial map one more time before the stakeout begins. He does a visual sweep to make sure nothing has changed since the aerial map picture. The store is rectangular, with double glass doors on the front, surrounded by glass windows. The window coverings are advertisements for gun and ammo manufacturers. It appears dark inside, and Spencer doesn't want to risk walking up to a window to peer inside.

Mac confirmed the surveillance with the owner and the local police again before they left for the stakeout. They are eager to capture this guy, too, but no one is more eager than Mac. Bobby still has not returned her calls. She prays he doesn't venture a trip up here tonight.

Each team takes up their positions, and promptly at 8:30, Spencer receives the first check-in. The road in front of the store is heavily traveled, even at night. No one speaks during the stakeout, as they just look and listen. A few times, they are on heightened alert when they hear a low rumble, but it passes their location. The team suspects a semi-truck in the area, but it cruises by the store and enters the interstate. By 2:00 am, the group gets restless.

Spencer asks Mac, "Do you want me to call it a night?"

"No. I am sitting here until dawn. Bobby would not have told me to be here unless he knew his dad would be here. You can ride back to Atlanta with one of the other teams, but I'm staying." Mac emphatically states.

"Well, I'm staying too. No way am I leaving you here to take all the credit when this all goes down," Spencer answers with a grin.

Mac's eyes droop when Spencer taps her arm. He points to the corner of the building just as Bradley whispers into the comms, "Heads up. A subject in dark clothes is approaching from the west, heading east. Stubin, he will pass by you, and then Spencer and Mac, you can pick him up from there."

Mac readies her weapon, stands, and waits for a visual. Finally, a man comes into view. He wears all black with a dark green army jacket and walks with a limp. In his hands, he carries four gallons of gasoline. Spencer steps out first, then Mac follows. They watch the man throw a jug toward the roof, but when he hears them approach, the jug misses its mark. Gilbert turns around, holding a lighter over the remaining three gallons of gasoline.

"Stand back, or I will blow us all up!" Gilbert yells as the lighter hovers over the already soaked rags. His eyes shift from one person to another as he works on identifying the leader. Old Army training is coming back to him.

Spencer tries reasoning with the man, even pleading, but it doesn't work. Mac steps out from behind Spencer and acknowledges the man. "Are you Gilbert Broth?"

Gilbert stops speaking and stares at Mac. She continues, "We know about your PTSD, Jeremy's death, and your kidney donation. Do nothing foolish, Gilbert. Bobby needs you, and he doesn't want to lose you. Think about what you have done, Gilbert. Don't make it worse. Can we talk about it?" Mac takes a baby step toward Gilbert. She wants to get close enough to knock the lighter out of his hand.

The other team members surround Gilbert without his knowledge. Gilbert concentrates on the flame leaping from the lighter and trying to hold the remaining gallons of gas. His arms quiver from the exertion. He sits the gas cans on the ground. Then he paces while the flame hangs over the gas cans. Gilbert walks by Baxter, who tries to tackle him. Gilbert screams and sidesteps the attempt. Baxter rolls on the ground, holding his shoulder as the lighter flame kisses the gas. One gas can explodes causing debris and embers to cascade in the sky.

Stepping away from the fire, Gilbert yells, "Move back, or I will torch this whole place!"

With the order, the team retreats but not too far. Mac continues trying to reach Gilbert. "Gilbert, please, do not start another fire. You've killed and injured too many people. This tirade needs to stop now. Will you help me?" Mac reaches out her hand to Gilbert, hoping he will take it.

A meek-sounding voice interrupts. "Dad, listen to Mac. She's trying to help," comes from the far side of the building. All eyes turn to Bobby.

Mac runs to Bobby's side as he approaches his dad. "Bobby, be careful. If he is having an episode, I'm not sure what he will do to any of us." Mac tries to keep Bobby behind her as a precaution, but he won't stand for it. He steps out from behind her and approaches his dad.

"Dad, please. Stop this. I don't understand why you are doing this. Can you put the lighter down and step away from the gas?" Bobby begs.

"No, I can't stop, Bobby. I must continue until all gun stores are out of business. This is the only way to protect you. If you hadn't been shot, I wouldn't be doing this. So, see, it is all for you, Bobby."

Spencer speaks this time, trying to console Gilbert into giving up peacefully, but nothing seems to satisfy him. It all goes back to the shooting. Not necessarily to Jeremy, but the wounding of his son. Gilbert only speaks of Bobby, not Jeremy.

Bobby walks over to Gilbert and asks for the lighter. Gilbert says no and asks Bobby to stand back. "Bobby, this is for your own good." Gilbert pushes Bobby backward against the team members. Everyone hits the ground as Gilbert rushes to the side of the building. He stands next to a gas can and strikes a flame from the lighter. Gilbert yells, "Bobby, I love you!"

The explosion shakes the building and leaves the team members momentarily deaf. Bobby rushes to his dad, hoping to pull him from the fire, but Tyrone reaches out and pulls him back. Gilbert screams in pain as the flames leap over his body. Once the pain becomes unbearable, he collapses and falls unconscious before hitting the ground.

Mac calls for the fire rescue squad and the EMTs that are on standby. They arrive within seconds of the call. They extinguish the flames, but they leave a charred wall of the store and Gilbert with severe burns covering 80% of his body. Rescue squad attendants stabilize him for the ambulance ride by covering his burns with sterile gauze and dousing him in saline solution. They administer pain medication through an IV to provide him some relief. Bobby rides to the hospital with his dad while Mac and Spencer follow. After the ambulance leaves, the fire department cleans up the gasoline from the roof and the store's rear.

A fire department medic examines Baxter's shoulder before letting him leave the scene. They place his arm in a sling and advise him to visit an ER within the next day or two in case he has a fracture. He grunts an acknowledgment.

Before Spencer and Mac leave for the hospital, Stubin advises the group to meet at the office for a debrief around two this afternoon. The somber mood carries its way through the group. They didn't want anyone injured, even if Gilbert chose to hurt himself. Now, Baxter might be out of work because of his shoulder injury.

We accounted for all the equipment, and no one fired bullets. But, when you play with fire, sometimes it gets dangerous. Stubin advises the group Agent Williams will be proud when he receives the report on this case. The night ends as the sun rises.

The next day Mac and Spencer debrief the agents in their mid-afternoon meeting since they got a late start. Gilbert remains in a coma, which helps in his recovery since he won't feel the pain from the burns. No man can endure that much pain and survive. Mac says goodbye to Tyrone, and they promise to keep in touch. Mac and Spencer spend the afternoon calling agents and gun store owners. They want them to know about the capture, so their lives can get back to normal.

Mac agrees to call Cliff with an update since she wants an update on Zac. Cliff is elated the team captured the arsonist and wants a follow-up if he survives his injuries. He wants to be present for trial if there is one. Zac's wife had their baby early yesterday morning. The doctors stopped the contractions earlier, but Zac had a terrible night, and they could not stop the baby this time. Their daughter is in NICU as a precaution. The doctors are optimistic she will be released within two weeks. Zac is stable and in his own room. So, things are better now. He thanks Mac for the update.

The next calls are to Leif and Toby. Both are happy to hear from Mac that they captured the arsonist. The doctors are releasing Leif by the end of the week to continue his recovery at home.

Spencer calls Agents Notting and Kimball with updates, and the capture pleases them, too. Both express a desire to partner with the duo in the future if the chance presents itself.

On her way home, Bobby calls Mac. He thanks her for trying to help his dad. Mac is grateful the ordeal did not cost Bobby his life. If Gilbert survives his injuries, he will spend the rest of his life in prison—if he doesn't get a death sentence. That could go either way for him, depending on the jury. The trial will be months or even years in the future, depending on Gilbert's recovery. Mac shivers when she remembers seeing Gilbert's burns along with the smell of burning flesh. That is something she will never forget.

Mac's night is pleasant. There are no thoughts of fires, only of Bobby and the long road to recovery for his dad if he survives his injuries. The night goes by quickly, and when the alarm sounds, Mac rolls over, envying those people who customarily get eight hours of sleep a night. She can't recall the last time she had a full night's sleep.

The team members sit at their desks, all pecking away on their keyboards. Stubin gave them a reprieve on the report yesterday. But today is a new day. The report is simple since they deployed no weapons. Those reports don't happen often, and when they do, it is a relief.

José and Bradley inform the team of Simon Burden's identity. They received information from the Swiss Bank holding the account, and it helped them confirm Simon Burden is Hunter Bows's son. He is twenty-two years old, and Caroline is not his mother. There were no family photos in the Bows' home that included Simon. Neither José nor Bradley could state if Caroline knew about Simon.

It seems Hunter set up the Swiss account for Simon as a way to keep Caroline away from the money. With Hunter's other accounts, they could have lived anywhere. José and Bradley feel Hunter's financials hold the illegal doings, but no one has found them yet, and now that Hunter is dead, does it really matter?

After the reports are complete, the group suggests a steak house for the celebration. Everyone agrees and stands to leave when Spencer's phone sounds a text tone. He reads it, and then he grins. Mac's gut tightens again. She contemplates skipping dinner but decides against it because she could use some downtime.

While everyone enjoys dinner, Stubin excuses himself from the table to take a call. Mac waits for his return while entertaining the other team members. After everyone finishes their plates, Mac glances up and sees Stubin walking back to the table with a grim expression. He sits down, looks at Mac and Spencer, and says, "You two have a new case."

New Release coming November 2021!

A brutal killer terrorizes a city as they carve odd shapes into their victim's torso.

Ellie meets Detective Harkins, an old friend of FBI Agent Watkins, at a crime scene involving blood spatter, Ellie's specialty. While Digger visits with Ellie, they put their weekend plans on hold as another bloody scene waits for Ellie's observation. Digger tags along as a courtesy but finds himself in the middle of his own investigation involving bone recovery and identification.

That's when the two cases collide. Can Digger and Ellie save their relationship when Ellie's old flame joins the hunt?

As the team works tirelessly to identify the killer, it proves difficult as the murders continue, and the killer sets his sights on those trying to end his melee.

Can Digger, Ellie and the team survive the attempt on their lives, or will the killer complete his picture with their bodies?

Other Books by A.M. Holloway

Promises of Murder (Sheriff Jada Steele Book 1)

Pieces of Murder (Digger Collins Thriller Book 1)

MOA (Mac Morris Thriller Book 1)

~~~~~~~~~~~~

Visit www.amholloway.com for new releases and to sign up for my reader's list or simply scan the code.

Made in United States
North Haven, CT
18 February 2023

32831362R00143